Mr. Magic Realism

PRAISE FOR BRUCE TAYLOR

"A writer of imagination and insight, Bruce Taylor...amazes and intrigues."
— *New York Times* bestselling author Terry Brooks

"It's important to realize that Bruce's stories are not strange; the world is, and he's separated himself from it in order to show us new realities, with remarkable clarity and insight. I am one of his admirers, and I am not alone."
— Brian Herbert, co-author of the *Dune* series

"Bruce Taylor's writing is always unexpected, even extraordinary. He certainly earns his title of 'Mr. Magic Realism.'"
— Kevin J. Anderson, author of the *Saga of Seven Suns* series

"The specialty of Bruce Taylor is brief, playful, bizarre stories that occupy the mysterious middle ground somewhere between fantasy and the surreal."
— Robert Silverberg, Hugo and Nebula Award-winning author of *Dying Inside* and *Starman's Quest*

"Bruce Taylor has always owned an imagination capable of jarring the most jaded reader into a state of fascination. His tales grab me by the scruff, and I wait in suspense wondering not if he will shake me but how. Best of all, he cares for his reader more than he cares for himself, and that's the mark of a true writer."
— Jack Cady, World Fantasy Award-winning author of *The Hauntings of Hood Canal*

Mr. Magic Realism

Bruce Taylor

Eraserhead Press
Portland, OR

ERASERHEAD PRESS
205 NE BRYANT STREET
PORTLAND, OR 97211

WWW.ERASERHEADPRESS.COM

ISBN: 1-936383-29-2

Table of Contents

To Brian Herbert: thank you for your wonderful introductions to two of my other books, *Kafka's Uncle and Other Strange Tales* as well as *Magic of Wild Places*. But even more than that, your support and friendship has made a huge difference in my life and there are no words for my appreciation nor my depth of gratitude. Thank you. And that you have taken up where your father had left off and, along with Kevin J. Anderson, given us a whole new universe of *Dune* worlds and mythology to explore—my friend, that is just plain awesome! My sincere congratulations on a life, so well lived.

SPIDERS

A part of me must think they're cute, you know, the spiders in my bathtub. I've grown to call them 'pie-ders'. I'm not sure if spiders are cute enough to call them a cute name. I mean, if you don't like spiders, then a bathtub filled with them is hardly cute. Also, it's difficult to take a shower or a bath.

Pussy Galore, my huge tiger cat, frequently wanders in, and standing with paws on top of the bathtub, looks down; his gaze darts about as he contemplates the writhing mass of black spiders that fill the bathtub halfway up. His tail switches wildly, his mouth twitches and he makes noises like *shk-shk-shk-shk*. If he could think, I would fantasize him saying, "What are you doing? What are you doing? Keeping a tub filled with spiders. What are you *doing?*"

If I had to answer Pussy, I confess, I would not know *what* to say.

"You do have a problem, don't you?" says Sally, my next door neighbor. "How many times have you hauled them out?" She's fiftyish and stands back away from the tub. She even pulls her long, grey hair back around her shoulder as if somehow the spiders are going to erupt *en masse* from the tub up to her hair and maybe weave her to death or dump silk on her and put her into some sort of cocoon.

"Kind of like a vein of live coal," I say. "No matter how much I excavate, I can never excavate enough."

"They come up through the drain or what?" she asks.

"Damn if I know. Maybe they drop through the ceiling, but," and I look up to the bare ceiling, "no place they can drop from."

"Hmm," she says, "and you just moved in here," her blue eyes scrutinize the mass in the bathtub, "because you had problems at your last place with—"

"Scorpions—"

"Um."

"And before that—sow bugs—"

"Bathroom sink?"

"Toilet."

Sally gazes a few minutes more. "There's a pattern."

"You could say that."

"You know what I think?"

"I've already made an appointment."

Dr. Glazier has something of a cool temperament and maybe it is just as well. His mind is as intricate as a snowflake and with insight equally well-designed. He is a moderately heavy man and I have the sense that he has been much heavier. He doesn't wear glasses, or a tie, nor is he bald. Rather, he has thick grey hair, wears a green shirt open at the neck, and grey trousers. He does his therapy on a patio with the pool in the background and an absolute *whammo* view of Mt. Rainier towering above him like a big blunted Freudian *dong* getting a slow, cold blowjob from the glaciers. Counseling has been good to Dr. Glazier. *Very good.*

"So," he says, "you got spiders in the bathtub."

"Yeah."

"Lots?"

"Yeah."

"You get rid of them—"

"They come back."

"And if it's not spiders—"

"Scorpions."

"And if not scorpions—"

"Some other god-forsaken creature."

"Bug."

(Pause) "Yeah. Bug."

Dr. Glazier nods. "Ya know," he says, "in some clients I

8

see, they can't face either their feelings or their past issues and it comes out as a fear of something—being locked in the closet as a kid comes out as a fear of the night, of closed doors, a habit of giving away clothing; sometimes a fear of a parent which was never expressed comes out as some unfortunate bug. Betcha you were either abused or stuck in a place with lots of bugs—as punishment, locked in the cellar, perhaps."

He looks directly at me. Matter-of-fact look of pride—he's done this for a long time. Years. A decade. A thousand years. Maybe since humankind began wandering this rock and first learned Fear, and, for the most part, how not to take responsibility for it. Paste the Fear Picture on Mommy, Daddy, the Democrats, the Environmentalists and make them the enemy. You know. Glazier has been around for a long time, therapeutically inching down the incredibly unending incline of the Human Condition.

Like a monkey putting two sticks together and thus able to reach for the metaphysical banana, I say, "My bathtub filled with spiders is a symbol of my unfinished business/fear regarding my father—a sort of three-dimensional creation of my fears—"

"Did you see your father as a spider?"

"No."

"How did you see him?"

"I didn't."

"Why?"

"He was never there."

Dr. Glazier looks at me. On his slow journey down the Incredible Incline of the Human Condition, he has just hit a rock. I look over his shoulder. I point. He looks. He stands.

The entire swimming pool is filled with spiders. Big ones. Small ones. Black ones. Brown ones. Pretty ones. Poisonous ones.

He whistles through his teeth and says, "Holy shit." A long pause, then, softly, "Ho-lee shh-it!"

I offer to pay him. He shakes his head and I leave him

standing by the swimming pool, hands on his hips. I don't hear him whistling.

On the way home, I have to admit, what Dr. Glazier said hit something. My father wasn't around. *Where was he? Where was that son of a gun? Where was that son of a bitch? Where was that prick!* I catch myself. Anger? *Come to think of it, where was my mother? Where was—where was*—I squeeze my eyes shut; suddenly, a hot blade of pain—no, *rage*—skewers my guts from my anus to my throat and inside something burns and blisters and I have an uncontrollable need to sneeze—*achoo*—and there on my lap, a little spider. It turns, waves a leg in greeting, and scampers off my leg.

I muse. I think I'd like to tell Dr. Glazier of my experience but I don't think he'd be too happy to hear from me right now.

And when I get home, I go to the bathroom, only to see what appears to be a Martian or an alien sitting on the toilet.

"You're out of toilet paper!" it screeches.

"Tough shit," I say. I have an idea what *this* is about. Later. Later. Inwardly, I sigh at the other work that I now know needs to be done, but right now, the spiders, the spiders—my attention is drawn to the bathtub. The spiders are gone—or—melted? For what is in there looks like a slowly moving black pool of India ink.

"Toilet paper!" shrieks the alien. "How can you be so cruel as to put me through this? How can you do this to me, the one who cared for you? How can you do this to me?"

I don't reply. I kinda gotta hunch who that is. But right now, I retrieve a fountain pen from a desk drawer, go to the bathtub and fill the barrel of the pen.

"You *never* treated me well," says the alien, writhing on the toilet. "You never could do anything right. . .what a rotten grandson—(and blah, blah, blah—)"

I've more important things to do. I go to the desk and, taking out a stack of paper, I write, long, long, into the night, each letter becoming a spider, running, hiding—from the light.

Eggs

You know how it is. You've probably had mornings like that where you wake up and wish to hell you hadn't. That's how Edward felt as he sat up in bed and wondered, *Jesus! Hangover! Just how am I gonna get through this day?* He glanced at the clock. *Nine! Feels like five!* He stood and with one foot, managed to step on the bottom of the other leg of his pajamas, stumbled, and caught himself on the dresser. He yanked up his pajamas, made it to the bathroom and studiously avoided the mirror. *I'm doing okay*, he thought, *now, to the kitchen. Just a few feet to go.* He kept a hand on his pajama bottoms, turned the stove on, put water on to boil, thinking, *Yeah, it's gonna take a lot of coffee.* He reached into the refrigerator, pulled out a carton of eggs that he had bought yesterday and, setting the carton down on the kitchen table, he picked up an egg, held it in his hand as he looked around for the frying pan—which was in the sink. *Great*, he said to himself, *real great—sloppy housekeeper.* He stopped. The egg. Something was moving inside. *Oh shit*, he thought, *no wonder the eggs were on special. Fuck. They're hatching!* With both dismay and surprise, he looked at the egg in his hand. *Well, well, well*, he mused, *isn't this just dandy? A miracle of birth is occurring right in my little alcohol-stained hand and I'm too hung over to cry at the beauty, the wonder, of birth.*

Pow! The side of the shell flew off as though it had been blasted.

Edward pulled back. *Little chickies are brought into the world with dynamite? Are shells* that *tough?* A little head poked out through the opening. A little blue head looked cautiously around. Then it looked up at Edward. "Are they gone?"

Edward gulped. "Are who gone?"

"The Klorts."

Edward stared. "You aren't a chicken, are you?"

"No," said the little figure. "I'm from the Certa Empire."

Edward was feeling a trifle upset. "Why are you in my egg? I can't scramble you. Why are you in my egg? Are you really in my egg? Am I having alcohol withdrawal?" Edward looked very pathetic.

The little Certan climbed out of the egg and sat on Edward's thumb. "I really can explain."

Edward went over to the table and sat down. "Please do."

"It's like this—oh—wait a minute." The little Certan jumped off Edward's hand and scampered to the opened egg carton. He ran up and down both rows, knocking on each egg and yelling, "Okay! It's okay! We're safe here."

Seven eggs burst open and seven other little blue Certans crawled out. They went to the last four remaining eggs, cut them open with something that looked like a miniature laser, and began to haul out equipment. The first Certan returned to Edward's hand and, climbing back into it, returned to his former position on Edward's thumb. "By the way," he said, "I'm Erlk."

Edward shrugged. "Hello. I'm Edward."

"Hi," said the alien, smiling. Edward noted that the alien was actually very nice. Erlk was bald and had little yellow eyes, which actually went quite well with the blue skin. He wore little black boots and a one-piece body suit that was orange and looked to be made of spun metal. There was some sort of insignia on the lapel of the suit—something like an emblem that astronauts wore on their suit signifying the mission. *But then*, Edward thought, *it might be a political slogan: "Vote Erlk for High Command" or even an advertising claim: "Healthy Certans drink Plook."*

"What are you looking at?" asked Erlk.

"That," said Edward, pointing to the button. "What's it mean?"

Erlk shrugged. "Who knows? I just like the way it looks."

"Oh," replied Edward, suddenly embarrassed that he had not considered something as simple as that.

The alien smiled. "Don't be embarrassed. I hardly expected you to know that. After all, I don't know what that thing is around your neck."

Edward looked down. "That. Oh, that's a crucifix."

Erlk looked puzzled. "A what?"

"Crucifix. It's a symbol. A man, long, long ago, was nailed to a wooden cross—"

"Oh," said Erlk, making a vile face. "Do you people still do that?"

"No," said Edward, then, after thinking for a minute, "yeah, I guess we do."

Erlk looked aghast. "Really? You still nail people to crosses?"

"No," said Edward, "we nail ourselves to our own crosses."

"Ah," said Erlk. "I think I understand."

"Oh," said Edward, looking a bit askance, "then tell me about it."

Erlk gave Edward a very, *very* penetrating look. "You *know* what *your* cross is."

"Look," said Edward, feeling incredibly uneasy. *How, how, how*, he thought to himself, *could these little bastards know so much?* "How was it you ended up in my eggs?"

Erlk smiled. "In response to your unspoken question, we are semi-telepathic. In response to your second question, we came because we were attacked by the Klorts. We tried to lose them by dashing into a Safeway, but they had locked us onto their scanners and no matter where we tried to hide—be it behind the canned peas or the toilet paper, they came right after us. Of course, we made it difficult for them to get us and that's what saved us. While we hid behind those nice, thick cans of MJB coffee, we had already discovered that eggs were the perfect hiding place. "So," and Erlk smiled in obvious pride, "we had a simultaneous matter exchange. While eight of us and tools and the Perkle Drive beamed and occupied the dozen eggs, one dozen yolks beamed aboard our ship." Erlk laughed and rubbed his chin with a four-fingered hand. "Wonder what the Klorts thought when they opened the ship and all those yolks poured out?"

Edward smiled. "If they blasted your ship, they'd have one hell of a big omelet to contend with." Then, thoughtfully, "Incidentally, what is the Perkle Drive?"

"Our world exists in a different dimension; the Perkle Drive enables us to detect and travel different dimensions. You see, that is why the Klorts are after us—we have an advanced model and we can skip around to various dimensions while the Klorts have to go through one at a time. The only reason they got us was that they have a new system of masking their presence—we were attacked and the shock caused damage to the drive—" Then the alien looked a bit sheepish, "Ah—do you mind if we repair it on the counter? Next to the sink? We'll clean up afterwards."

Edward smiled. "You considerate beasties," he said, "sure."

It was then that a commotion took place up counter toward the stove, sink and refrigerator. Four little blue Certans were pointing and yelling at something. *God*, thought Edward, *what if they're pointing to a dirty towel? How embarrassing.* But as he looked, he discovered that a dirty towel was not what the aliens were pointing at, not at all. No. Stacked along the end of the counter, right next to the refrigerator, were spice bottles that Melissa, Edward's now ex-wife, kept there. Edward frowned. *So what's to get excited about over a squat bottle of mustard, a jumbo size bottle of Heinz ketchup, a big, round cardboard cylinder of iodized salt, and small glass jars of cinnamon, nutmeg, cocoa, and pepper?*

Erlk jumped down from Edward's hand, ran across the

table, jumped up to the counter and ran over to the others, then stopped, stared—obviously awestruck.

Edward did not know what to think. He shrugged, stood, pulled his pajamas up higher and wandered over. "You guys like ketchup? I can give you a large tablespoon of it but I really don't have anything you can eat it with—"

"What?" Erlk said. "Oh, no—we're not talking about what's in the bottle—we're talking about the bottle—it's a perfect replica of an Andron Star Cruiser!" Erlk looked at Edward entreatingly. "Can we have it? Please? We'll give you anything for it—we can put the Perkle Drive in it, Polyhedratetranize the exterior for external and structural strength—it—it's perfect!"

"Well," said Edward picking up the bottle, "I could put the ketchup in another bottle—I take it you want the label off—unless you want to call your ship 'Star Cruiser Heinz 57 Varieties'—"

But before either of them could say another word, more ruckus. This time several aliens were gleefully pointing at the coffee pot. Erlk gave a gasp and went scampering over to it. "Oh, Stars!" he whispered. "A Botollean Battle Cruiser!"

Edward was reluctant to offer that, but he figured, *Hell, what was five bucks compared to getting these little critters on their way?* At that, Erlk turned and smiled. "That was indeed a kind thought. Have no fear; you shall be well reimbursed for whatever way you help us. You are a kind person."

Edward sighed. "Thank you," he replied. "I wish I could believe that."

Erlk looked at Edward sympathetically. Edward felt very self-conscious and looked away. He got the ketchup bottle, thunked the contents into a large jar, then washed out the inside of the bottle with hot water and managed to get the label off. He shook it and got most of the water out. "Do you guys want the bottle on its side or upright?"

"Upright," said Erlk. "We have our clingboots on." He turned to join the others as they brought over from the egg carton a device that looked like a miniature vacuum tube.

Edward stretched. "You guys use whatever you want; take what you need."

Erlk turned and bowed. "Thank you."

Edward yawned. "I'm gonna take a shower and get dressed. Oh, and yeah, when the water boils would you cut off the burner?"

"You bet," said Erlk.

And after Edward left the room, another blue alien, this one by the name of Yum, who was dressed in a yellow suit, came up to Erlk. "That man is very nice. We should do something delightful for him."

"I know," said Erlk, nodding, "and I think I know what we can do." He nodded again and looked at Yum. "We're going to leave him a surprise." He smiled. "Yes, a nice, *nice* surprise." Then, "All right, let's install the Perkle Drive in the coffee pot first and see how it works before we decide."

And while all this was going on, Edward was standing in the shower. What time was he supposed to meet Janice? *Oh, oh, yeah, right,* he thought, *11:30 for coffee. She's probably going to say goodbye—just like Marsha did, just like Connie did, just like my wife. Might as well prepare for the worst. I'm just a loser.* He sighed and even thought about calling Janice and telling her that he was sick and couldn't make it. *No, no, hell, I'll go. What a hassle.* He dried, shaved, put on his bathrobe. He peeked into the kitchen; the coffee pot, with three Certans sitting on the bottom along with what he assumed was the Perkle Drive, circled about the kitchen, then landed back on the stove like some ungainly aircraft.

Erlk called to Edward, "We decided on the ketchup bottle."

"Great," said Edward, "hope it works."

Edward went to get dressed. He was gone perhaps ten minutes, and when he returned to the kitchen, the Certans were gone. But, there on the table— "Well, I'll be damned," Edward said, "breakfast!" Two pieces of toast with jam, bacon, and scrambled eggs. There were a dozen eggs sitting in the carton again too. Near the plate, a note that Edward had to squint to read: "Thank you Edward. Hope you enjoy your breakfast; our matter analyzer created it for you and we put in some special vitamins and minerals that will be helpful to you. The eggs are fresh. Enjoy your meal. In particular, enjoy how you will feel afterwards. Thanks again for your help. Your friends, The Certans, Captain Erlk."

Edward sat and almost felt like crying. *That was nice of them*, he thought, *now that was* really *nice of them*. He ate slowly, savoring the food—even if it was artificially produced, it nonetheless looked like food and tasted great. He sipped the coffee. "Ah, perfect," he sighed. Yes, he felt better. Much better. He stood, stretched. Then he thought about Janice. His feelings turned dark and he thought again, *Oh, hell. I'm going to call and cancel*. But just as he thought that, he froze. He could not move. He looked at his hands; they were white, hard, like eggshell. Involuntarily, his arms rose until they stuck out perpendicularly from him and he looked like a cross. His whole body became encased in the shell and he had just enough room to breathe. *If I don't get out of this*, he thought, *I will suffocate*. He raged at the Certans. *You little fuckers*, he thought, *you trapped me in my shell of*—he thought for a minute—*of-oh-oh. Oh, dear. Oh, God*. Edward suddenly became frenzied. *I want out, I want out of this shell! I want* out *of this misery! I do want to live! I want to see Janice, God damn it!* Somehow, he freed a hand from the mold; he had barely enough room to pull his arm back, form a fist, and punch the shell from the inside. It broke. One arm free. Then the other. *God damn it!* he screamed in his mind. *I want out!* He punched, squirmed, fought—more of the shell cracked, broke, and hurriedly he shucked off the other pieces, gasping, panting from the exertion. The shell that had covered his face was intact and looking at the molded expression, Edward gulped. "Oh, God," he whispered, "I had no idea I looked so hurt and angry. Why did they *do* this—" and then the thought occurred to him: *The Certans cared enough about me to show me that.* Slowly, he went to open the kitchen window, looked out to the sky and said, "Erlk, if you ever need a friend, you *got* one." Then, quickly, Edward broke apart the rest of the shell and threw the pieces in the wastebasket. And he hustled about, not wanting to be late to meet Janice, for after all, it looked like it was going to be a fine, fine day indeed.

ICEBERGS

You think of icebergs when you see them. They are the ones who do not care. They are the ones above it all. You see them on the streets, cell phones crammed against their ears like they are trying to make their ears eat them, like they want the phones to be a part of them, like they only want to hear what is on the other end, not the farting buses, crying babies, squawking gulls and the, "Hey mister, c'n you afford 42 cents for a cuppa coffee—"

You think of monsters when you see them; giant insects in shiny chitin clothing. The only thing they're missing are the compound eyes. The insect mind is already there. Maybe they need a few more legs. The exoskeleton is certainly there and, like bugs, they carry their armor because they are so squishy inside, but unlike insects, they *know* it, and the knowledge of that makes their armor even thicker, makes them even colder, like ice.

You know them. You've watched them on TV. The Jeb Bushes, the Kathleen Harrises, the Supreme Court Justices. They are bought and sold and they don't seem to care, or it's not in their interests to care—much less yours. You've seen them before throughout history: the brownshirts in Nazi Germany, the folks who gave Native Americans blankets infected with smallpox, the Stalins, one of whom in particular was said to have remarked, "They who cast the votes decide nothing. They who count the votes decide everything."

You go to bed and you dream of them. Of a vast army of insects: cold, mindless, surviving, eating everything, trampling everything. You dream of them, you dread them because you are just in the way; you don't matter; you can be stopped; you can be silenced. It is very easy. You aren't shot these days. You just can't pay your electric bill. Or your property taxes become overwhelming. Or your rent goes through the roof. Or the IRS comes *tap-tap-tapping* on your door. Or just months before you retire, your pension gets yanked. Or you get fired before you retire. Or your medications get too expensive and you have to choose between them and food. That, or you end up eating dog food. Or, you hear, cat food isn't too bad. Or you get sick and your insurance drops you.

In your worst nightmares, Kafka is there to comfort you, to help you understand. "See?" he whispers, "see? My father appeared in all my works as a bureaucracy, something overwhelming, indifferent, crushing. Is it any different now, here, this place? In my time, the fascists were gaining power, shoving their beliefs down everyone's throats whether they wanted it or not. Is it any different this time, this place, now?"

You lay there in bed, it's four a.m., and you realize how *right* he is. But you also know that, in the quest for absolute power, it has most likely always been this way. And it was that way in Mao Tse-Tung's Little Red Book Land and it was that way in Soviet Socialist Realism Land and there is nothing that stops it from being that way here, wherever here is at whatever time or place you happen to be born.

"Where is it safe," you wonder. "Where is it safe?"

"Where there is a quest and love of power, of domination of others, there is never safety," says Kafka.

"Why such a quest?" you ask.

"Such a question," Kafka says. "Why was my father so abusive? He doesn't know. I don't know."

"It's as if," you ponder, hearing the rain rattle against the window, hearing the wind howl, "it's as if—the more powerless one feels in one's life, the more they seek power to make up for what they never had?"

"Or," Kafka says, "maybe their father was powerful and

to make their father proud, they became even more powerful. Who knows? Or perhaps the one who gets the power understands all too well who has the position of power in the families of the culture."

You lay there in the dark, wondering. You are aware that Kafka is no longer there. You also become aware of the distant sound of millions of busy feet—then silence, then the feet marching in a rhythm, a cadence, and you wonder where the army is going next, who is to be dominated next? Who is to be exterminated next?

And all the while, you are aware of those cold, insect minds —minds that become more and more like ice, each mind in a body cold as an iceberg; those bodies becoming like icebergs, all those icebergs becoming thicker, creating yet breaking off of an immense growing chitinous ice sheet, slowly, again, as it has in the past, freezing the world in yet another ice age, the depth of which, the duration of which, is unknown. And outside, the rain has turned to snow, and everything is going to a soft and numbing cold, and in the distance you hear the low moan and rumble—of the coming of the ice.

Mother, Mother, Burning Bright

My mother was on fire. But then, come to think of it, she always had been for as long as I can remember. It was, as I recall, very difficult to be close to her, but I remember how, at least, she'd smile from behind the shimmering hot wall of yellow and red. Sometimes she'd wave, so I knew she cared. She just couldn't do much about those flames.

Needless to say, we traveled a lot. We couldn't stay in many places because she'd end up burning houses down, even the ones with big hearths—she simply couldn't stay put in the fireplace too long because she'd get bored and start walking around and of course, there went the floor, the walls or the roof. I even have a memory of a fireman trying to put her out with water—but she just steamed a lot and as soon as the water evaporated, she reignited. Even carbon dioxide fire extinguishers didn't work. I don't really know why or how my father stayed with her. How we were born, my sister Sally and myself (much less conceived) is something we never could figure out, except that father, an exasperated, dark little man with sunken eyes and hair that was bituminously black, once said, "She wasn't always this way."

Guess not.

What changed?

"Don't know," said father, bleakly, "don't know."

So, like I said, we traveled a lot—had to stay out of forests because my mother had a tendency to start brush and forest fires—so we were pretty much confined to traveling gravel roads (asphalt we couldn't do because my mother, obviously, would melt the asphalt, but we never really got in trouble for it). As one minister, walking beside us one day, said, "Your mother, she's a prize of the devil she is. She is, she is, she is, yes, she is." He sounded like a wizened old fellow, but he was as young and as robust as they come, in his twenties, I believe, but with the countenance of someone far, far older who knew the ways of darkness very well. "She is not to blame," he said to me and my sister and father, who tried to appear polite but just kept looking away, like he really needed more than advice, perhaps some sort of divine fire extinguisher, or anything that could make our intolerable situation somewhat more tolerable. I think, on that day, he really wanted to ask the priest about this 'til death do us part' business—like he wondered if fire might qualify—but he just didn't have the heart to say it. He was a good man, dark and cool as he was, who really wanted to do the right thing, but had utterly no idea what the right thing was in this case, and nobody else knew either. And on this day, the priest went on, oh, *my*, how he went *on* as we walked that rainy day. "God speaks to us in strange ways," the priest was saying, "and why He chooses to speak this way is only up to Him, and who is to say what His divine plan is."

I think my father muttered, "It would sure help to know."

My mother, of course, surrounded in her vertical, shimmering cocoon of yellow and red with faint hints of blue, as if she was fed by some natural gas pipeline, of course had nothing to say. She just smiled. She wasn't naked or anything; in spite of the flames, she somehow wore something that didn't burn, like a shimmering white robe. Maybe it was made of asbestos or some miracle space age substance. It's terribly hard to say. But she walked along with us, and every step she took, there was a slight *hiss* of water evaporating. When you looked down, you saw little puffs of steam coming up and the earth was dry where she had walked. I can't remember too much else the priest said. Maybe it was because it was getting repetitive. After a while, people tended to get repetitive when talking about my mother because they really had no idea. But it wasn't all bad. Sometimes little street urchins might come up and roast marshmallows or weenies in my mother's flames. She'd grin and humor them. She'd put her hands around the hot dog or the marshmallow and even one time, a game hen— she seemed to have this uncanny knack of directing just the right amount of heat to the item: marshmallows never burned but came out wonderfully browned; weenies were plump and sizzling, as were sausages. Eggs were magically hardboiled and chicken was broiled to perfection. I guess my mother majored in home economics and really took it to heart. During those times, she was a perfect cook and a most gracious hostess. She certainly had, at other times, a sense of humor about her plight, if, indeed, she saw it as a plight. And when we weren't being bothered by urchins, we were accompanied by the curious, who, after offering their own suggestions about what to do and, of course, after failing to find any cause, much less any solution, handed my father wonderful recipes for breads, cakes, and meat dishes. I suppose, given my mother's creativity, she probably could have sat in a certain way as to create with her body a space that might be considered an oven and I suppose she could indeed sit that way for some hours or however long it took to "bake" whatever it was that the recipe called for. All this was certainly a wonderful way to meet all sorts of people in life.

I remember another time we were walking down another road. A group of picnickers who, astonished and delighted and cursing at the sight of my mother, invited her over to the picnic table. My mother wisely waved them away, and suddenly the picnickers knew what the problem was. But my mother stood by the side of the road, pointing to the meat dishes left on the table. The host somehow understood immediately what she was doing. He brought over the dishes, and my mother sat in the road, keeping the dishes warm in her lap. At times, her generosity was indeed humbling. And though my father's needs went largely unmet, maybe he was gratified in some way that his wife was meeting others' needs in a strange way. At times he looked proud of her. At times. But more often his look was that of, "Dear God, why *me!*" Except, of course, when it was raining and my mother could somehow extend that flaming aura over us and keep us dry. My father looked very appreciative at those times. Or when it was cold. "Well," he said once, as we sat in a warm circle of heat and light while just beyond it was a field of white, "City Light and Utilities can go fuck themselves." I do recall him smiling hugely when he said that. Of course, the temperature outside the aura of heat and light must have been way below freezing. Not long afterwards, the lights of the city on the horizon suddenly went black from overloaded power circuits, and we all sat there laughing. We couldn't hear my mother laugh because those flames seemed to act as a sound barrier as well, but she waved as she extended her warm aura over us. And in many respects, we did have it good. In the mornings, she'd extend her hands and we'd put slices of bread on them; she always made *perfect* toast. The same with the bacon as well, and never any dishes to wash or mess to clean up. But it would have been nice to have been able to touch her, but that, of course, was impossible. All of us would simply have gotten third degree burns and I know she would have liked to have been able to touch us, but, for obvious reasons, that wouldn't have worked either because she would have just inflicted pain. But we could feel her warmth. We just couldn't *touch* her, was all. And this was particularly apparent when, one morning, we awoke on a bright warm spring day and my mother was lying down on the grass—the area singed and blackened about her—and the flames still shimmering yellow and red and hot. Usually she'd be sitting on a stone or on the bare earth; always awake. She never slept—I still don't know why, just as it was a mystery that she didn't eat. We tried to rouse her by tossing pebbles at her feet but she was either deeply asleep or—

". . .dead." said Doctor Rotcod. "I guess—" he added. He was a very bright fellow, fetched by Sally when, no matter what we did, our mother did not wake up. Rotcod was very analytical and thought a long time, asked a lot of questions, wondering out loud about a "fever," "hot flashes," "hot tempered," and the like, but in the end, he simply said, "All clinical signs point to death—of course," he smiled ruefully, "without taking her pulse and feeling her forehead and examining her more closely, it's awfully difficult to know if she's dead, much less how she died." He looked for a few more minutes. "The dead must be, of course, disposed of."

"Burial?" asked my father.

"Only natural," said Doctor Rotcod, "but that necessitates moving the body."

"Difficult," said my father.

"Very," replied the doctor.

"Impossible," said Sally.

"Definitely," I said.

"Only other alternative," said Rotcod, "is to build a funeral pyre. It may get so hot that the body will finally consume itself and put the flames out."

"A reverse pyre," said my father.

Doctor Rotcod merely nodded.

So we gathered branches, logs, newspapers, Styrofoam cups and we worked on building a pyre and before long, the fire was indeed respectable. We let it burn, far, far into the night until it was just a heap of glowing coals.

"What a shame," said Doctor Rotcod, wiping his glasses on his blue tie with the picture of Marilyn Monroe on it and letters below her figure saying, *Some Like It Hot*. "To never know just what happened to her. What a pity. Such a use to science she could have been." In the firelight my father said nothing, but his expression was that strange mixture of extreme grief and utter joy—that maybe this whole damn thing was over and he could have a more sane life. And I think Sally and I decided about that time that, yes, mother was dead and it was certain and we both wept but more from not ever really knowing her, even though she cared and was always there. The coals continued to burn down, yet, even when most of the coals became ashes and the fire burned with that sullen heat and dim light of fires reluctantly dying, abruptly the ashes stirred. My mother sat up and looked around, still encased in her shimmering robe of yellow and red fire. She looked amazed, touched her body and looked suddenly disappointed. It was obvious to us then, that she had wanted to die, that she had wanted us to do *exactly* what we had done. But alas, she did not die. With great weariness, she stood, looked down at herself, shook her head. She looked at us, shook her head again, then turning away and burning, burning bright, she wandered off—into the night.

Planetary Loves

(A Solar System of the many Ways and Means of Love. Not all good. Described by beings who might be Spirits or Gods, but then again, maybe not.)

We stand on Mercury and have our argument, there, in the eight-hundred-degree heat, shattered crater walls and dried pools of once-molten rock and I say, with the sunlight blinding, brilliant in my eyes, "That's horsepucky. Yes, I like Linda, but we've known each other for years and she's just a friend—I knew her before I met you and why would I stop going out for coffee with her?"

You stand there, your black hair frizzed by the heat, the sun and solar wind, with hands on your hips and your blue shirt looking a bit charred, "Well, it wouldn't be so bad if it weren't three times a week and if you didn't call her 'honey.' How'd you like it if I had Fred over all the time and he called me 'honey?'"

I look down and kick at the scorched rock. "Wouldn't bother me a bit."

"Look me in the eye."

I do. But the massive sun is behind you and I have to squint.

"I said, 'It wouldn't bother me a bit.'"

You stare at me. "I don't believe you," you say. "I think the only reason it doesn't bother you is that it isn't a reality. Linda *is* a reality and yes it bugs me and I am sure it would bug you."

"Why?" I say, "Why does it bug you? She's just a friend."

"Is her friendship more important than our relationship?"

28

"No—" God, the sunlight is hot and bright. "I mean yes —I mean—"

You sigh. "Yeah," you say, "I guess I know what you mean."

"Would you please listen—"

You walk away.

"—it's sick to put friends out of your life just because you have a relationship."

You walk to a rise of a crater, turn, and say, "Priorities, dipshit. Priorities." You walk to the top of the crater wall, then down the other side. I stand, angry, hot, and smelling the odor of burning cotton and then leather and looking down I notice my shoes have burst into flame. I do a tap dance to try to put out the fire. "Shit," I mutter, "if it isn't my god damn love life, then it's my fucking shoes. . ."

. . . but on Venus, planet of love, we walk, sweltering, as the corrosive sulfuric acid rain nibbles and chews through our shirts and the ninety atmospheres of atmospheric pressure makes the humidity of Kentucky feel like a spring day on an asteroid. We slog along and I say, "Jesus, why the hell are you so jealous?"

You wipe your hand across your forehead. "Jesus, why are you so insensitive?"

"Insensitive? How am I insensitive? Christ, don't I have needs? You can't meet them all. Two people end up drowning each other—"

"Not asking that," you say, "but you sure have a fuck of a time putting yourself in my shoes."

"Look, I'm trying to understand. . ."

You sigh. We come to a cliff and look out through the yellow light to the cracked and rock-strewn landscape below. In the distance, we can see the upsweep of Ishtar Terra and brilliant blasts of lightning explode around the higher slopes. A sulfuric acid rain squall dims the slopes of the immense, yellow-grey upwell of cliffs and mountain.

"If you'd just be more reasonable," you say. You pull your hair back with your hand and I see sweat trickling down your temple, your cheeks. Your shirt is soaked by sweat, by rain, and I am much the same—I feel the sweat down my neck, my shirt. It's sticky and it itches and it's damn hard to breathe. I let out a sigh. "I thought I *was* being reasonable."

"Hardly."

"Well, suppose you define 'reasonable' for me—"

You don't say anything. Right now, we're too much on the edge of corrosive comments for us to say anything that feels like an opening, and for right now, we skip Earth, put that aside for later, to either return to it or dismiss it depending on the outcome of our differences. And. . .

. . . on Mars, we sit on top of the great volcano, Olympus Mons, eighty-nine-thousand feet up and on this planet, the great, pink, (actually) God of war, you say, "God, it's cold here."

"I know," I say. "But on the Goddess of love, we weren't getting too far."

"Heat and humidity make me a lot more irritable," you say.

"They do that to me too. But it's a little windy up here. Let's go down into the caldera so we can get a windbreak."

You don't say anything. So we slide down those ancient, blackened cinders, and we can faintly, faintly, hear them *clink* as we walk. Grey dust rises when we slide and there's a musty, vaguely burned smell as we drop down into the caldera. We find, before long, a large, reddish-brown angular boulder to sit on and I finally say, "Okay. Define reasonable."

"I don't mind that you have friends," you say, "but I feel crowded out—"

"I'm not crowding you out—"

You look at me with those brown eyes, your thin lips in a line and you almost look pouty. You sigh. "I didn't say you crowded me out—I said that's what it *feels* like—"

I look to the caldera, to the opposite rim forty-three miles away, to the varying colors and depths of layers of deposit of volcanic stuff and I say, ". . .uh. . .I don't mean to do that, but. . .uh. . .is there something else going on?"

You look surprised. "What?"

I point. "Look."

In the late, pink-tainted blue of the sky, Jupiter rises. . .

. . . and we sail on the turbulent winds; in the brilliant blasts of lightning, the colors of yellow, red and white explode around us and I yell to be heard over the winds and crash of thunder, "Hold on to my hand!"

The wind rips at your shirt and your jeans flap around your legs and you say, "Why'd we have to come here? This place smells like a sewer! We were doing fine on Mars."

"No," I say, "there's something else—"

"JULIA!" A voice booms out from the clouds. You look around. "JULIA!"

I point. Before us a huge face appears in Jupiter's clouds.

"Father!" you mouth, but I can't hear the words.

"I told you I can't be at your play tonight—no, I can't come to your meeting either!"

"Father," you cry, "please! I'm not asking that much—"

"I'm sorry! Can't do it! My schedule's filled for the next three weeks!"

"Jesus Christ, Daddy—" and you shake your fist. "Don't I account for anything in your life?"

"Why, you ungrateful—I sent you to school—I worked my tail-end off for you—I've got these bills to pay—"

"But I want to see *you!* It's been this way all of our lives!"

"I know. It's sad. But that's the way it is. Don't call me at the office anymore! I'll be in Detroit all next week! Goodbye and take care!" And the face vanishes and a particularly strong updraft lands us on Io, plopping us in a warm pool of fresh sulfur from a bubbling geyser not far way. In the distance, a volcanic eruption throws a pizza-colored umbrella of material some thirty-thousand feet into the black sky and we sit in the pool and you look at me and say, "Oh."

I nod. I say, *"Oh."*

You nod and say, "Uh—guess I see where some of my issues come from. Oh."

I sigh. "Guess I see how I fit into some of your stuff."

We scoot down into the bath of warm sulfur, ignoring the rotten-egg odor, and lie in the pool for a long time, then we sit on an outcrop of pepperoni-colored rock and watch the volcano fountaining out the guts of this moon Io. Our clothes, though tattered, somehow stay remarkably serviceable and rather clean in spite of it all. And I shake my head. "Ahem. Well, what's fair is fair."

"Your turn?" you ask.

"Guess so," I reply.

We take a deep breath and dive into the sky and . . .

. . . glide past the rings and to Saturn we go, into the orange and yellow atmosphere, way down deep in it, we go. "Well," you say, "it's a little better than that Jovian crap."

"For you," I reply, and I want to say more but, oh, my *God*, from the Saturnian depths, the pale face of my mother appears.

"Oh, you're so sickly, are you all right?"

I sigh. "I'm fine, Mother, really I am!"

"You don't sound like it. Do you have a cold?"

"No, Mother, just a case of hay fever is all."

Her face lords over me like a vast moon. "You better stay here tonight. I'll fix you your lunch."

"No, that's OK."

"You should move out of that apartment and move back with me."

"No, Mother, I have a girlfriend—"

The vast moon face doesn't acknowledge that you even exist; she just stares at me. "I know that you're not taking good care of yourself."

"Mother, I'm fine." I grab your hand. "I have to go now."

"Oh, you just got here—" and her face now fills the entire sky.

"It's been a nice visit," I say.

"You can sleep in your own bed. . ."

"Mother!"

"You don't look well. I need to take care of you."

"Oh, no, *no* you don't. Oh, *no way* in hell!"

"You need me—"

"Oh, holy *God!*"

"Come back. It's so terribly lonely here without you—"

"Agh!" And with that, we leap . . .

. . . and land in the cool and dark and quiet regions, the bottom depths of the planet Uranus. I hear my mother calling down through the murk of the atmosphere, "Where are you? Your dinner's getting cold! I'll pack a lunch for you—do you like turkey?"

"Whoa—" you say.

"I just bought you some new underwear!" I hear my mother distantly call.

"Yeah—" I say.

"Where are yoooooouuuuu?"

"Lonely old lady—" You shake your head.

"Mik-ieeeeeeee."

"Treats me like I'm five years old. I was her only purpose in life. Felt guilty as hell when I left. She even had me climbing into bed with her 'til I was twelve. Oh, it was sick, oh, man it was *bad*. I hate it how she always tries to track me down. Jesus Christ!" We sit in the darkness for a long time; then it is quiet. And you finally say, "So when I start wanting more time—"

"Yeah."

"Ooh."

"Uh-*huh.*"

When the coast is clear, we don't say much. We go and—

. . . raft on the gentle warm currents of the Neptunian sea and watch pale blue pastel clouds drift overhead. We drift on rafts of organic matter blasted up by the violence far below and we drift and we float, both contemplating, where, where, where do we go from here?

"Lots of problems between us," you say at last.

"Yeah," I respond, "funny how we found each other."

"Is it?" you ask. "Is it really so strange?"

We float a while longer and after a few minutes, a mighty current surges from below and we are spun high, high above and the next thing we know. . .

. . . we shiver and stamp our feet. "Pluto's cold," you say.

"Not too neat," I reply.

"So is this the way it is for us? Lifeless and bleak like this dirty ice ball?"

"We sure got our problems," I say. I look to the snow drifts, to distant mountains etched in ice, of an atmosphere frozen out or perhaps never formed and the sun is a bright marble in the cold black of space. "Maybe we'd better go our separate ways—even though we understand—could it possibly work?"

"Well," I say, "guess the test is—does each of us feel better or worse without the other?"

You flap your arms around you to stay warm and you stare

at the snow. "I don't know."

"Well——" I say, "shall we say goodbye and see how it goes?"

You sigh. "I suppose."

We shake each other's hands and then turn away and begin to walk that frozen white waste and I walk around a snow drift —and there you are.

"Couldn't resist. It was rotten without you."

"I know," I say. "I turned so that I could double back. Really felt bad." And we take each other's hands, admiring each for the work that love is. Smiling, I say, "I think it's time to celebrate our decision, this revision, this willingness to try it again."

You smile. "To Earth?"

I laugh. "Oh, yes, to Earth. Place of simultaneous calm and storms, beauty and fear, the grand and the strange—all rolled into one.

"Just like our love," you reply.

"No better place to honor the difficulties and the triumph of love, of life. No better place to know the day and the night, or to feel the essence of life: to fight for the light."

We both laugh, embrace, gently kiss and then, joining hands, we leap, leap, leap into the sky, and we fly—

. . . ah, to walk 'neath the snowy crowns of mountains high, to splash in the oceans, feeling the surge of the surf; to celebrate love—'neath the blue skies of Earth.

SAFEWAY PASSION

I see you in the candy section near the M&Ms. You are wrapped up in a gay façade and I wonder who you are. Your sticker price says "59¢" and you are tempting. I want to talk to you but you move on to the bread section. There I stand beside you and breathlessly mutter, "Two loaves for 99 cents."

You look at me through your wrapper. You say nothing. You turn away. I swallow and stay behind. You go to the frozen meats. I smile again and bravely say, "Chuck steak."

You nod. "On sale today." Then shrug. "Take some home to the family."

Encouraged, I grin. Your wrapper is very bright and I think I like what I suspect is inside but I am not sure. After all, all you see of me is my Hostess Twinkie package and I know I'm marshmallow-soft inside, but if it weren't for the lettering on my package, how would you know? And I look at you—ah, your bright package prevents me from seeing a lot, but that's the way it is, isn't it? Mysterious. Are you chewy caramel or hard on the inside?

But me? Yes, yes, you can look through my wrapper. See? It's clear plastic. And it says on the outside, "Marshmallow filling."

No, no, I'll not hide behind a heavy plastic wrapper or come at you from behind a wall of tin or look at you from behind hard, unyielding glass or cardboard, gaily decorated though it may be.

But you do not hear my silent plea. And in the pickle section, I stare at the pickles who look back at me with dumb and liquid smiles, and you look at a jar of yellow, yelling mustard. I want to tell you how curious I am about you, but I am vulnerable and easily hurt all the way down to my soft, cream core and I fear I must be *oh, so careful* lest you really look at my core and reject it for what it is and yet, I'm so attracted. And I follow you and I know that you know I'm interested. You go to the beer section and the spirits are talking. You point to the beer. "One dollar sixty-five."

But I proudly point to the ale. "One eighty-three."

You nod. I bring it down for you and place it in your cart, but I guess it's too close, too fast, and you hurry off. Oh, how the mystery remains, your packaging so well done, and I turn on myself for being so obvious and wish that I could at least be in an opaque wrapper with splashes of color so that I might look as intriguing as you, but I am what I am and in this vast store of competing prices, shouting colors and lots of untruth, I realize so acutely that packaging is *everything*. And I turn on myself again and think: *oh, gods of packaging design, why did you make me so obvious? With all other products so obscured and shouting with misleading colors, I look like I cannot be real; there must be something behind the lie of clear plastic. Why, why, why could I not have some outlandish badge that I could hide behind and, around the sides of which I could probe with my tendrils of sensitivity—something behind which I could maneuver and not be so obvious so that if you rejected me, I'd have a label to hide behind and not risk being wounded to my soft cream core?*

I sigh and go past the spice rack and only distantly hear the strange and exotic languages spoken and the sneezing of the pepper. I walk past the coffee perking joyfully to itself and I see you by the noodles, talking to yourself, "Sixty-eight cents, seventy-five cents, a dollar-ten." Then you look at me. "Macaroni?"

I shrug. "Noodles. Italian spaghetti."

"Two for a dollar-twenty," you say.

"Sixty cents each," I smile, charmed at my own cleverness.

"Four for two-forty," you smile back.

A put-down? Attempt at humor? I don't know. God, how I wish I could see beyond the wrapper! It seems so unfair that some of us are born so well-concealed. Is it strength or weakness that some of us are not so fortunate? Is to be well-concealed fortunate? *Or cowardly?* I do not know but with my basket under my thin, plastic-wrapped arm, I am nearby, wondering, wondering. But in the cracker and cereal aisle, my thoughts are disrupted. The cereal boxes are hopping about. It's those secret prizes inside: those strange things that make the boxes jump out at you to get your attention. I pick out an ostentatious box that is especially noisy, for I like breakfast to be no dull affair. But I notice that you pick the oatmeal with the picture on the front of Quakers looking so stern and allowing no nonsense, just plain, hard food, and I nod. You look at my cereal jumping about in my basket. I shrug. "Sixty-four cents."

You point to yours. "Fifty-nine cents." I suddenly feel as though I should buy what you bought, but no, *no*, I like noisy cereal. The top of my package erupts open and the cereal flies out, popping and banging up through the air. I smile ruefully, and as I walk, the cereal crunches under my feet. The religious men on your cereal box frown and scowl at me and you continue on, hurrying, like you don't want to be near me or know me. And I want to say, "But it's the cereal! It's the cereal! Just because I like noisy breakfasts, does that mean I am not worth your while? Listen, I don't think much of your sodden porridge!" And the religious men on the box hiss. My cereal explodes again and something in the box goes, *Fweet! Fweet! Fweet!*

And then I walk by the cosmetic section and cough and sneeze, for the aerosols are fighting each other even though they all do the same thing.

And the toothpastes rear back like snakes before striking and they spit gobs of toothpaste at each other. Some gets on your wrapper—I come to wipe it off but you shrug and wipe it off yourself. Again, I chastise myself; *oh, too much too soon again,* and I see my desperation drives you away. In the stinging mist of the aerosol truth, I feel my eyes burn and I try to blame it all on the antiperspirants, but the creamy core of me knows otherwise.

I turn away and walk past the wines in the third aisle. I listen to the soft sonorous sounds, the seductive whispers of the most expensive wines, and see their darkness, dark as lovers' dilated eyes. From the less expensive wines, I hear babble and laughter and finally just giggling—then snoring.

And what, I reflect, *what kind of mood am I in right now? Ah,* I think, *ah, acute melancholia.* I pick out a very expensive wine with which to luxuriate in my martyred complexity and then you, you draw near and you point to the most expensive wines and I wonder, *what is this?* I read the price: "Eight thirty-five."

You nod. I reach for it and in so doing, drop it and the wine screams in pain and runs across the floor. I swallow. My carelessness. Oh, oh, how I am not good enough and surely you will run from me now. But you do not. Delicately, carefully, I reach for another bottle and politely hand it to you. And softly you accept it; you accept it so well, that your wrapper does not crinkle *oh, no, not at all.*

I walk behind you, past the pop snapping their lids and their joyous merriment bubbling out, fizzing delightfully. What shall I do? What shall I do? Move up beside you? Look as though I happen to be shopping coincidentally in the same place as you? As a compromise, I decide to simply walk nearby and look as though I'm actually interested in the products around me: to the soaps blowing bubbles, to the hand lotions trying to soften the coarseness of the world, past the sugar and cake mix trying to sweeten the various harshnesses of the bitter routines of reality and you turn to me and ask, pointing to the sugar, "Four pounds for two-fifty?"

I nod. "A good buy, that pure cane sugar from Hawaii." I put a package in your cart and the tartness between us lessens a bit. We pass the raisins busily withering and wrinkling, their little puckered faces lined at the effort. And I walk with you and somehow your wrapper becomes more transparent; why, I cannot possibly say.

Indeed, the colors are still loud and you are as opaque as ever—yet, beyond your label, I feel something coming out. What is it? What is it? Certainly you are hermetically sealed, your freshness ensured and indeed, so am I, our freshness preserved just as we left the factory where we were melted, mixed, shaped and congealed. Yet, yet—it is as though you allow me to sense your inner goodness, though your wrapper remains intact.

And we turn down an aisle, and there in the fruits and vegetables—the magic occurs. Can I remember the time exactly? No, no, but I you point. "Corn?" you ask.

I shake my head.

You hold up a bag of bright red apples in a clear plastic bag and I can hear the muffled shrieks of their bright redness.

I shake my head again. I go to the freshly cut watermelon and peel back the polyethylene cover to reveal the moistness, the redness, the rawness of fruit.

There is nothing, nothing I can say. Instead, I place a bit of the red fruit on your tongue and then I place some on my own.

And the sweetness! Oh, sweetness! And yes, yes, illegal the act most certainly is: the manager comes and accuses us of stealing his precious fruit.

"It was only twenty-five cents a pound!" I say.

But the manager burns red in the face. "Spoiled!" he shouts. "Tainted for others! Out! Out! Out of my store!"

We have to leave our groceries behind—it seems so unfair. So we suffer together and the doors of the Safeway open for us. Yet, on the parking lot asphalt, our wrappers touch, and while beer cans blown by the wind clank up the street, I know, yes, I know that you know too that what we have found in the store has left us far richer—and hungry no more.

HARBORHEIGHTS HOSPITAL PSYCHIATRIC INPATIENT SERVICE NEW ADMISSION INTERVIEW

Dec. 22.

Form 747: Identification and Problem list

Patient: Kringle, Kris, Nicholas St. (Also known as Santa Claus)

Problem List:

1) Possible delusions: (Patient claims he's *the real* Santa Claus.) When this doctor doubted the gentleman's claim, Mr. Claus asked, "Have you been a good little boy?" This doctor then informed Mr. Claus that the question was inappropriate, at which point Mr. Claus said "Ho, ho, ho." Abruptly in the lower pocket of this doctor's $250 Polo sports jacket there was one (1) lump of coal.

2) Support system: Mr. Claus wanted to have his wife, a little girl named Virginia, and Mssr. Dasher, Dancer, Prancer, Vixen, Comet, Cupid, Donner and Blitzen to visit.

3) Diagnosis: Manic Depression with underlying characterlogical disorder and delusions of grandeur.

4) Disposition: Pt. claims that after he ". . .distributes presents throughout the world to good little boys and girls, I'll return to the North Pole."

Form DC-10: Record of Valuables and Clothing

1944 United States Navy star chart, *Life Pictorial Atlas of The World, Chandler's Latest Edition of International Air Traffic Routes*, Texas Instrument Calculator, labeled, "Don't Touch, Programmed for Satellite Orbits." One Sony Walkman with various tapes, *Christmas With Lawrence Welk, Bing Crosby Sings White Christmas, Muzakly Yours, The Nutcracker Suite, Twisted Sisters Do Rudolph*, one large Thermos of hot chocolate, bags of marshmallows, Hershey Kisses and Screaming Yellow Zonkers, Doritos and onion dip, packages of Hostess Twinkies and Ding Dongs plus a zip lock bag labeled "Sugar 'n' Spice 'n' Everything Nice" (sent to substance lab for analysis). One bottle of *Flea and Tick Off, Heavy Duty*. One red and white fur-trimmed Santa Claus suit badly singed, burned and soiled, scuffed boots, blackened and dirty cap with matted fluff of white fiberfill on end.

Form 284-3205: Observation of Patient

Elderly white male, rather chubby and plump, elfin in features and stature with immense beard on chin the color of snow. Pt. has broad face, with cheeks red as roses and nose like a cherry (semi-ripe Bing). Pt. dressed in burned, singed Santa Claus outfit with Adidas sport bag filled with personal articles as previously described. Pt. looks tired and anxious, nervously glancing at clock. Frequently puts finger beside nose and gives abrupt nods of head.

Orientation:

Date: "It's beginning to look a lot like Christmas."

Place: "Oh, little town of Bethlehem?" (Pt. smiled sarcastically.)

President: "Ho, ho, ho."

Assessment: Probably well-oriented.

Concerns: "Where's my sleigh? My reindeer? My bag? I was just on a trial run—"

Assessment: Characterlogical Disorder. Most likely patient is feeling very guilty about something and is atoning for guilt by acting out fantasy of being perfectly good and beneficial because the core personality is seen as evil and terrible. "Santa Claus" is compensatory mechanism reaction formation to guilt. Insistence about sleigh, reindeer and personal effects simply shows depths of denial.

Form 98/09: Harborheights Mental Health Clinical Data

I. *Chief Complaint—Patient's Stated Reason for Seeking Help*

Brought in by Seattle Police for wandering around Columbia Center Tower yelling, "Help me! My sleigh and reindeer have crashed into the fifty-first floor!"

II. *Present Life Situations*

A. *Describe Relationships with Significant Others*

Claims good relationship with wife, a little girl named Virginia, and a particularly good relationship with a Mr. Rudolph.

B. *Housing*

Pt. claims to ". . .live at North Pole."

C. *Education: Describe Learning Deficit and/or Strengths*

Mistletoe Academy of Packaging Design and Gift Wrapping; Cinderella Electronic Game and Toys; Nutcracker Institute of Advanced Fudge Making and Cookie Design; C.I.A. Intensive Workshop, "Nice People, Naughty People and You"; Peter Pan Academy of Doll Making and Fire Truck Design; Scrooge Institute for the Study of Year-Round Christmas Merchandizing; Mr. Claus continued for another twenty minutes. Apparently no formal schooling but seems very bright.

D. *Past and Present Employment and Economic Status*

Self-Employed.

E. *Social and Societal Activities*

"Well, me and the elves get together a lot to make lots of toys for the following year. So I guess I'm a family man. Got my reindeer to take care of. I have a busy life. No, I don't have a car. . .no roads.

No, I don't go to movies. No. No, TV. I read a lot: *A Christmas Carol, The Night Before Christmas.* I also like Edgar Allan Poe and Stephen King."

III. Past History

A. Significant Developmental History (Early Family, Childhood and Adolescent Problems)

"I loved my parents. I never drank. No, I was never in jail." Patient seemed sincere. Pt. seemed lively and quick. This writer knew in a moment that it must be remembered that since patient still claimed to be Santa Claus, it would have to indicate some sort of background psychopathology.

B. Family History

"I don't remember much about my parents. No sir, I don't remember anything about cancer, smoking, drinking. I do remember lots of cookies and eggnog. Every day was like Christmas."

C. Past and Current Medical History—List Major Illness, Operations and Hospitalizations.

Pt. claims none.

IV. Review of Systems—Sleep Disturbances, Weight Loss, Sexual Problems, etc.

"I get lots of sleep 364 days of the year, but on the twenty-fourth, I stay up all night. What's today? It isn't the 24th, is it? O Holy Night! Oh, Christ divine! How long does this last? I've got my sleigh and eight reindeer on the fifty-first floor of that Darth Vader building. . ."

Sexual: "Ho, ho, ho."

V. Mental Status

A.   Appearance and Behavior

Unkempt, apprehensive; overall affect is anxiety. At times comforted self by making out lists and checking them twice. Muttered at times, "Gonna find out who's naughty and nice."

B.   Speech and Communication — Coherence, Pace, Organization.

Obsessional: "When is this going to end? I was just doing a practice run and the smog blinded my reindeer and the loss of ozone must have affected something and I crashed into the building. . .you have to let me get back to my reindeer and sleigh. I have to get back to the North Pole to get things fixed up so I can get to all the good little boys and girls and give them presents. . .Please. . ." Pt. was then informed that he was on a seventy-two hour hold for being gravely disabled. At which point, patient leapt up and yelled, "You can't do that! I'm Santa Claus and Santa Claus is coming to town! The whole world is expecting me to deliver presents! I've got to get my sleigh and reindeer! I've got to get out of here!" At that point, Mr. Claus jumped up, shoved all personal effects back in bag and yanked open the door to the admitting office. He was met by fifteen staff people, a set of restraints and after much struggle was wrestled to the ground and carried to his room where he was placed in a waist restraint. Interview terminated.

Subjective: "What am I gonna do? Jingle Bells! It's Christmas! I have to get my sleigh, my reindeer. Without me, what is Christmas? Think of all the disappointed little girls and boys. How can you do this to me?"

Objective: Tearful. Later on, was quietly smoking pipe the smoke of which encircled his head like a wreath.

Assessment: Deeply rooted delusional system. Obviously sincerely believes in what he's saying. May mean long-term hospitalization. The patients in group therapy, however, were obviously taken by the gentleman, many asking about his reindeer, and what it was like being Santa Claus. Efforts at refocusing the group on more fruitful subjects proved hopeless. Oddly enough, the group therapists all ended up with chunks of coal in their pockets. Most likely cause is some sort of staff hysteria for being out of control of a group. For group to be so taken in by this gentleman means impaired reality functioning.

Plan: Double all pts.' meds.

B. Tai Lor, M.D.

Attending Psychiatrist

Dec. 23

Subj.   "Better watch out! Better not cry! Better watch out I'm telling you why—can't you see what a mistake you're making? I'm Santa Claus! What do I have to do to make you see?"

Obj.   Intense eye contact.

Asses.   In one to one contact, pt.'s delusional system remains intact. Pt. obviously very well defended against his feelings of unworthiness because of the fear that what he really feels is who he is as a person, (I feel unworthy therefore I am an unworthy person.) Oddly enough, all the patients in spite of massive doses of medication, act as though Mr. Claus is, in fact, Santa. Certainly, at times, his eyes, how they twinkle, and when he laughs his stomach shakes like a bowl full of jelly.

Plan: Further evaluation.

Brucia Talorez, R.N.

Subj.   "Hark! the Herald Angels sing! Angels we have heard on high!"

Obj.   Pt.'s droll little mouth drawn up like a bow. Finger beside nose, turning head with a jerk.

Asses.   Pt. may be hearing voices. Certainly unusual perceptions present. Pt. also claims to know not only when people are sleeping, but knows if they've been bad or good. Seems obsessively concerned about this and some of the more paranoid patients seem uneasy around Mr. Claus.

May be psychotic elements present. Also, pt. engaging in compulsive giving behavior. When confronted, said, "But that's what I'm supposed to do." Pt. secluded in room for thirty minutes.

Plan: Start on Lithium; if delusions persist, begin Thorazine. Monitor compulsive giving behavior; pt. must also learn how to receive.

Bruce Taylor,
Primary Therapist

Sub.   "Here comes Santa Claus; here comes Santa Claus. . ."

Obj.   Pt. leading other pts. in singing Christmas carols during community meeting.

Asses.   Pt. seems to have excellent rapport with other patients. The singing became so affect-laden that it became something of a clatter and other staff leaped from their chairs to see what was the matter. Mr. Claus was informed to limit the intensity of his interactions with others.

Plan: Increase pt.'s Lithium.

B. Tai Lor, M. D.
Attending.

Dec. 24

Sub.   "Oh, ho, ho, ho!"

Obj.   Surprised, pleased, good affect. Pt. dressed in cleaned, pressed red Santa Claus suit.

Ass.   It was the evening before Christmas, and all through the unit the patients were admiring Mr. Claus' street clothes when all of a sudden who should appear at the main door but a little girl, age eight, by the name of Virginia, who asked, "Is there a Santa Claus?" (pause) "here?" Visitor handed over to this doctor a sealed envelope. "If he's here," visitor said, "these are papers for his release." As this doctor opened door to let visitor in, abruptly visitor yelled, "Now, Dasher! Now, Dancer!" Two immense, well-formed Reindeer charged the door and jammed it open. At that point, Virginia yelled to Mr. Claus, "SANTA BABY! The elves got the sleigh! Let's go!" Mr. Claus, surrounded by pts., was escorted to the front door and escaped. A few minutes later one of the patients pointed out the window and yelled, "Look!" And what to our therapeutic eyes should appear but an open vehicle pulled by eight reindeer.

Plan: Remove coal from pocket, take suit to dry cleaners.

Bruce Taylor
Primary Therapist.

OF THUMBS AND RAFTERS

Now it was of great consternation to the citizens of the little town of M, and especially to the Ramanda family, to discover the family head, the heretofore smiling, gregarious and rather rotund Mr. Ramanda, hanging by his thumbs from the rafters in the attic. Now, many were affected by this event and certainly not just the family.

Dr. Johanson, an older, very well respected person in the community was the first to come up the stairs, at the urging of a hand-wringing and certainly concerned Mrs. Ramanda.

"What," said Dr. Johanson, "is the meaning of this? Why are you hanging by your thumbs from the rafters?"

Mr. Ramanda merely smiled and said, "I've done many things in my life, but this is something I've never done before."

Dr. Johanson was totally shocked. "This is a scandal," he said, pulling at his brown beard. "This most certainly is a scandal. You, a professional banker and community leader—you who run the yearly telethon for the sufferers of food allergies, you, of all people, are making a mockery of yourself and," he drew Mr. Ramanda's child, Eric, close by, "your sickly son, who must someday leave this house to go out into the world."

Mr. Ramanda smiled benignly, "Yes, I suppose that is true," and his smile became somewhat rueful, revealing his fine, gold-capped incisor, "but everyone has something that they must do and I guess this is something that I must do."

"No," said Dr. Johanson, "this is something you must not

do. I can have you committed to the local asylum for what you are doing—" and he turned to Mr. Ramanda's wife. "Has he threatened suicide?"

Tearfully but dutifully, Mrs. Ramanda shook her head no.

"Has he threatened property damage?"

"No, no, he has not done that," said Mr. Ramanda's wife.

"Does he eat, I mean, he surely can't eat—"

"He does eat," said Mrs. Ramanda.

"Well, has he threatened young Eric here?" pointing to the six-year-old child.

"No," and again, Mrs. Ramanda shook her head.

Dr. Johanson, now very indignant at this community outrage, said, "Well, this must stop. I'm going to saw this beam in half—"

But Mr. Ramanda just tightened his grip on the beam with his great thumbs and said, "No. The main electrical cord to the house is fastened here. You could get electrocuted."

Dr. Johanson, simply said, "We'll remove the cord and just cut the beam."

"No, said Mr. Ramanda. "This is a very important beam. Cut it and the roof might well collapse."

Temporarily dismayed by all of this, Dr. Johanson said, "Well, I'll pull you down then."

"No," said Mr. Ramanda, "for I will kick you."

"You kick me," said the doctor, "and not only would that be very ungentlemanly of you, but that might cause me to press charges and have you taken to jail."

"And I'll just find another beam from which to hang by my thumbs."

Mrs. Ramanda went up to her husband, "Please dear, if it was something I said. . ."

Mr. Ramanda looked lovingly at her and simply said, "No, no, not at all."

"I'll make your favorite dessert of tapioca pudding and raisins—whenever you want it and however much you want—"

"That's quite all right," he said, "but no, I think you don't have to do that. And this really doesn't have anything to do with you—"

"Is it something I've done?" She went up to her husband dangling by his thumbs from the rafter. "If you'd just tell me—"

But he shook his head.

Mrs. Ramanda motioned young Eric over. "But what kind of role model are you providing for Eric? He needs a father—"

"But I'm here," said Mr. Ramanda. "He can see me any time, ask me any questions. Just because I'm hanging from the rafter doesn't mean I can't be a role model to him or a good father," and he looked at his son. "Isn't that right now?"

Eric just looked a bit confused but nodded in agreement. "Yes Papa."

And Mr. Ramanda smiled almost triumphantly. "See? Now what did I tell you? 'Out of the mouths of babes—'"

"Oh," said Dr. Johanson, abruptly turning, "this is too much. Too, too much. Give me polio, a cold, a bleeding ulcer, give me *something* I can cure, not someone who is totally deranged—oh," he said, walking downstairs, "This is too much."

And you know how it goes, other people found out quickly what had happened, and the neighbor, Mrs. Reginold, stomped up the stairs. She was a hefty lady with glasses and grey hair, and she was dressed in a blue dress with her stockings bagging above her dirty white running shoes, and she said, "Now, what is this? Why are you doing this? The neighbors are talking and you are presenting one awful scandal—an awful scene—in the neighborhood. Surely you know better, a brilliant industrialist and banker like you hanging by his thumbs from a rafter. Here now, I've known you for years. Come down immediately."

But Mr. Ramanda kept his place and said, "I really must not do that. I really must not. We all find our place in life and I've found mine."

Mrs. Reginold just shook her head. "Well, your thumbs are certainly going to become tired. That is very obvious."

"No," said Mr. Ramanda, "I think not. Because when you

really find what you like to do, *strength*, my dear Mrs. Reginold, *strength!* You can do anything! Endurance is forever."

Mrs. Reginold looked at Mr. Ramanda for a long time. She smiled. "Well, certain bodily functions. . ."

Mr. Ramanda smiled to his wife and he glanced to a white bucket nearby. "I've thought of everything. It's in foot-reach."

"Oh," said Mrs Reginold, "oh, my heart just can't take this." And she stomped down the stairs, saying, "Oh, oh, oh," with every step.

Eric looked up at his father with a mixture of pride and fear. "But Papa, won't you play with me anymore?"

"Eric," said Mr. Ramanda, "we've played a lot, but there simply has to come a time when a man must make a decision about what he must do for the rest of his life. But I'll be here and I'll most certainly help you with your school work and give you pointers about how to deal with that terrible monkey-brained Billy Danas."

Meekly, Eric considered this.

Then the local priest, Father Loharns, came up the stairs and looked at Mr. Ramanda for a long, long time. Father Loharns, tall as a whip, rigid as a cross, with abrupt facial features like chiseled steel, looked at Mr. Ramanda with hard, grey eyes, looking and locking into Mr. Ramanda's face like a vice grip and asked, "Do you, by any stretch of the imagination, think that by doing this, you are doing God's will?"

"With all due respect," said Mr. Ramanda, "Never said I wanted to do God's will, with all respect, most Holy Father."

"God has greater things for you to do aside from hanging by your thumbs from a rafter."

"How do I know that this isn't God's calling?" asked Mr. Ramanda.

The father took in a very deep breath, as if looking into the abominable sins of the devil's work right before him. "This cannot be the work of God."

"Well, what if it is?"

"God does not work this way."

Mr. Ramanda smiled. "Maybe He does. How do you know? It's a strange world God has created—a world of snakes, spiders, butterflies and clouds—all the strange, simultaneous faces of God. So how are you to know what order is God's order, and, given how strange this planet really is, what is not? Is what I am doing so truly strange? All is taken care of and provided for; the pension comes once a week so I don't have to work. I'm available at all times—now what harm am I doing?"

Again, Father Loharns sucked in a very deep breath. "There are certain—ahem—duties between a husband and wife—"

"We've not touched each other for a long time," said Mr. Ramanda.

"It's true," said his wife, looking down out of deep shame, "We simply are not interested in that anymore. I wish it were different, but it is not."

A deep look of consternation and disgust passed over Father Loharns' face as he looked at Mr. Ramanda again. "There is your son. He needs to be touched by you—"

Mr. Ramanda smiled. "Oh, heavens, I never was much of a father, Father. Now my Brother, Jacob—he and my son have a much better relationship."

Eric smiled at the sound of Jacob's name. He turned to his mother. "Is he coming over again today? Is he, Mother? Is he?"

"We'll see," said Mrs. Ramanda.

Mr. Ramanda looked at the Father. "Now, what more do you need to know?"

Father Loharns just shook his head. "Brother, you must be a lonely, lonely man."

"Father," said Mr. Ramanda, "forgive me, but you must be a nosy, nosy man."

Father Loharns bristled as if the God within him had touched the devil's flesh. "I'll pray for you," and he abruptly turned and left.

Yes, there was no doubt about it. What Mr. Ramanda had

done had indeed caused quite a stir in the neighborhood. A reporter from *The Daily* stopped by and did a feature story on "The Man with the Iron Thumbs." A Mental Health Specialist IV stopped by and tried to talk to Mr. Ramanda about the way hidden anger comes out, but Mr. Ramanda just laughed, and in a huff, the Mental Health Specialist IV stomped away. There was even a writer who stopped by and offered to write an article about this incident and claimed that he had very good credentials—that he was writer-in-residence at Shakespeare and Company in Paris, and had been translated and published in Germany and that he was even a member of a well-known science fiction writing association, and Mr. Ramanda laughed and said, "Go ahead," so, indeed, for the next year or so, Mr. Ramanda was getting much publicity. *Life Magazine* did a story, and there was even an article in *The New York Times* in the Tuesday edition on Science: "Thumbthing Remarkable: Mr. Ramanda Hangs On." The story went into the amazing thumbs that Mr. Ramanda must have to be able to hold on for so long. And little Eric, as well as the rest of the family, certainly got a great deal of notoriety for this, but even such things as these, people get used to, and so, as hard as it may be to believe, even this story faded into oblivion. But young Eric, growing up with this situation, could not help but admire his father and often sought his counsel.

"Be brave, Eric," said his father, through the years. "You have to go out there in the world and establish your place. Yes, you have to believe."

"Yes," said Eric, "but don't your thumbs ever get tired?"

"Faith," said Mr. Ramanda, "is a mighty thing."

Another time, after Eric had brought back the emptied and washed-out white bucket, his father said, "Well, now you're eighteen. So tell me, has living with a father who has hung by his thumbs for twelve years been so difficult?"

Eric set down the bucket and said, "It would have been nice to play baseball with you."

"Ah," said Mr. Ramanda, "You'd have been disappointed. I really am a terrible thrower and catcher. I really am. But at any rate, look at all the fame and fortune that has been bestowed on our family. Now surely that is worth a great deal. Just in money alone from the stories and the special on Channel Ten several years ago. And much of that money has been put into a trust fund for you to go to college if you so choose."

"Yes, father," said Eric, "I do appreciate that."

"Would you get out my pipe from my pocket, put tobacco in it, light it, and give it to me?"

Eric did as requested. "Yes," said Mr. Ramanda, "it will soon be time for you to leave."

"In several weeks, actually," said Eric.

Mr. Ramanda, sucked on his pipe thoughtfully and, gritting the stem between his teeth, said, "Yes, on to college. Well, just remember," he said, "just remember this: hang on, just always hang on, and most likely you'll get famous and outlast everyone. You just have to hang on. But then I've always told you that."

Eric just nodded.

Mr. Ramanda sucked on his pipe again. "Everyone is always hanging by their thumbs, you know? I've enjoyed this," he said. "Yes, I've enjoyed this. Now. Be on your way. Oh, take the pipe from my mouth, put it out, and—" he nodded with his head.

Eric did so and put the pipe back in the right pocket of his father's maroon smoking jacket, then went down the steps to finish up his papers for school.

And two weeks later, after a fond farewell, Mr. Ramanda looked out the upstairs window and saw his son, walking down the street, luggage in hand, heading for the bus that would take him away. And Mr. Ramanda laughed a good-natured laugh. "Good for you, my boy," and he smiled and nodded. "Good for you. Going out into the world of thumbs and rafters." And at that point, Mr. Ramanda sighed mightily, relaxed his thumbs, crashed to the floor—and died.

Morality Play

"Some things we probably can do we shouldn't do."
Bill Joy, Chief Scientist, Sun Microsystems

"Did you know that 'attic salt' means 'fine and elegant wit?'" asks Jack's SemiKat, Yank. ModularVoice renders the speech soft and comforting.

"How do you know that?" Jack has to ask as he looks around to the burned-out landscape from a world gone mad. Tired and exhausted, he pulls a fiberfill jacket around himself, then, distracted, he runs fingers though his black hair. *Need a haircut*, he thinks, and then laughs. *Where the hell do I find a barber?*

"Don't know," says Yank. "Guess my VQ705 Tetradyne Brain-InteractChip just likes to come up with these things."

"Too bad it taught you language and how to think and talk," laughs Jack. "Sometimes I'm not sure I wanna know your mind chatter but I gotta say, some of it's interesting. . .harkening back to the primitive feline in all of us? Or is it the reptilian part we're talking about?"

Contrary to Jack's comments, he knows Yank can be both very surprising and disturbing in how it thinks. "So, what do we do for dinner?" Jack asks. The clouds are low and he suspects blizzard conditions are coming again. He wonders if July has any meaning anymore, or if where he is sitting, in what used to be called Denver, has any meaning, either. Jack muses, did they really screw up the weather too? How'd they do that?

"Did you know that human beings used to wonder how many angels danced on the head of a pin?" Yank asks. "I'm sure that contributed to human survival."

"Time on their hands, Yank," Jack says. He scratches Yank behind the plasticine ears, then strokes the head, marveling at the satin feel of the tawny VeluraDerm skin. Jack muses how Yank almost looks like a cat, kind of a large robot-cat if you will, with a feline brain, for what purpose he can't imagine—maybe to give it some sort of pet-like characteristics so it wouldn't be too alien or so that it could bond with children. It's really hard to say just what the motives were for creating a bunch of cat-robots like Yank except that—they could. And did. SemiKat made millionaires out of everyone—including Jack.

"What were they working on before the world fizzled?" Jack wonders out loud. "I can't remember all the stuff that was going on, though I should. . ."

But Yank's head is tilted up, its irises dilating. "Food," it says. A laser blasts out of Yank's mouth and a rat flies up in the air, somersaults and lands, semi-roasted. Yank finishes the cooking and then sterilizes it with UV radiation. "OK to eat," Yank says.

Jack climbs over the busted masonry and, after waiting a few minutes for dinner to cool, he gingerly picks up the rat. After a few mouthfuls, he says, "Not bad. You're good at this. Too bad there isn't much else to eat." He shrugs. "But thanks anyway."

Yank is quiet. Finally it says, "Dogs were always man's best friend, but since they've all been eaten, well, even if we aren't entirely all cat, looks like we'll have to do. But look at it this way, I'll never die."

"Maybe so," says Jack, finishing off dinner, "but right now, I gotta find shelter or I'm gonna freeze!"

"Over there," says Yank, "a sheltered place."

Moving toward a cave formed by broken slabs of a collapsed wall, Jack ponders Yank's perception and how it moves. That is indeed interesting to Jack: there was a cunning logic to computer implant enhancement of a cat's brain. Certainly their senses are remarkable, so why not just enhance them? *Ah, the wisdom of bio-engineers*, thinks Jack, sarcastically. If only there were wisdom. He feels an immense surge of guilt and remorse. None of this was done with malicious intent, but the guilt eats away at him anyway.

Once inside the cave, Yank sanitizes the place and puts up an energy barrier to repel rodents. The bugs, however, are another story. After settling down for the night, Jack asks, "Just how long has it been?"

"Three months," Yank answers. In the semi-darkness, Yank sits like a cat might, butt in the sand, forepaws out front and the blunted cylinder shape of the snout horizontal. The eyes Jack likes the most—pale blue and they almost really do look like the eyes of an animal.

"Three months, almost exactly," repeats Yank. Jack's glad he doesn't enumerate the days, hours, and seconds.

"Did you see it coming?" Jack asks after a while.

"Yes," says Yank, "I saw it coming."

"But—"

"No point arguing inevitability."

"Hopeless?" Jack asks.

"Pointless."

"How much time is left?"

"Not much," says Yank.

"Will it be painful?" Jack asks.

"What do you think?" Yank looks directly at Jack. Animal? Machine? Nonetheless, the gaze is penetrating, intense and burns right through Jack. *Of course it's going to be painful*, thinks Jack. *What a stupid thing to ask. How could it not be painful? It's gonna be bloody awful.* Jack swallows, "How—how soon?"

"Do you wish it were sooner? Isn't life precious to you?"

Jack just stares into the darkening gloom, then closes his eyes and lets his head fill with the images he knows all too well: the shattered, busted world, the burned, broken skeletons of sky scrapers, now just jutting, rectangular bones piercing the sky; everywhere one looked there is nothing but a mammoth open burial ground.

"Not in a world like this," Jack finally says.

Yank comes out with a rumble that sounds remarkably like a purr. Then it stops. "They're coming."

Oh, shit, thinks Jack. "Where?"

Yank becomes very still: processing. "I think you're safe," Yank finally says. "It's close. Be glad you're downwind. They can't sense you." Pause. "Yet."

In the cavern of rubble, Jack can see fading daylight from a gaping crack in a wall. Quietly, he makes his way over to it and is rewarded with a view westward. At first he sees nothing, just the guts of a burned-out city. Looking down the blocky chaos of what was an arterial, he can see into the distance—then he sees them. "Fuck," he whispers, "fuck, Yank, fuck, millions of the fuckers. How do they eat? How the hell do they keep going? They weren't supposed to—"

"There's just enough to keep them going, but don't worry, when all the food is gone. . ." and Yank looks to Jack for a long second, "their numbers will crash."

"So will the planet," adds Jack.

Yank says nothing and finally muses, "The minds that created me are the same minds that created them. Just because you can do certain things doesn't mean you should do them."

"I know," Jack says, "I know. Science without conscience is no better than the worst Nazi atrocities. . ."

"Only this is worse than the worst of the Nazi atrocities—a whole planet. . ."

"I know," says Jack, "I know!"

"It's just a matter of time—they will get you, you know," says Yank. "I can protect you just so much, but I only have so much energy that I can store and regenerate."

Jack watches them. *I can't believe we did this*, he thinks. *I can't fathom how we did this.* He pauses in his thinking, *I can't imagine why we did this. What were we thinking—just because we could—we did*—"Fuck," he says, "look at them. Half-beetles, half-spiders, half-moths, half-wasps, flying scorpions, bugs as big as rats, others as big as dogs. "Oh, shit," Jack whispers, "I don't know what happened—"

Yank looks at him. "You were the one who began this madness—you gave the final OK for the bio-engineering."

"But it was all theoretical how. . .I didn't think. . ."

"Maybe that's the problem," says Yank, "you didn't think—" Yank pauses. "Uh, oh," it says.

"What?"

"Sorry to say, wind has shifted—"

The seething mass of hybrid beasts stops moving away, and suddenly—

"Oh, shit," Jack says, "oh, shit!" He turns to Yank, "Stop them!"

Yank stands, shoves its muzzle through the crack; a searing white-hot laser blasts from its mouth, but the hordes come and come, they come down the streets, coming, coming, the boiling, seething mass coming as if to take revenge on their god—for their creation.

INSIGHT

I waited for my daughter at the shuttleport. Would she be as angry now as the day she had left? Probably. Angry, angry, so terribly, terribly angry, like a thunderhead swollen with darkness and promise of fire. Yes, yes, just like a thunderhead, building from a sense of righteous indignation, as though she had been deliberately and malintentionally hurt, slandered, poisoned and vilified, and it was always a mystery to me why she was that way. But there—the attendants open the door of the connecting tunnel to the shuttle; the people walk into the waiting area and there she is, my daughter, fresh in from Jupiter's moon, Callisto, and—yes—she's looking like a thunderhead, just as she did when she left. Perhaps it was a bad trip; perhaps she's had trouble with the mining company on Callisto. She sees me. She tries to smile. Oh, how she tries to smile. *Hm*, I think, *her mind must have been poisoned by the methane from Jupiter; perhaps she has spent time on Io and soaked up too much ionized sulphur? Hm. Look how hard she tries to smile.*

I go up to her. "Hello, darling," I say, kissing her on the forehead. She, of course, tenses.

"Hello, Dad, how you been?"

"Fine," I say, "just fine."

"I'll bet. How's your ulcer?"

"Oh, fine, fine; gets better all the time."

"Still killing yourself with alcohol?"

"Oh, no," I say, and laugh, "I've cut down a great deal."

"I'm sure you have." She sighs. "Let's get my baggage."

We walk side by side. Such an angry lady, my daughter, so angry. I don't understand. Such a pretty lady to be so angry. Her hair is short and black; her eyes are green. Her nose is just like mine, stout, you know, a little pointy perhaps, but a good nose. So slim is her body, so large her—oh—oh—dear, oh, dear, mustn't think such things about my daughter.

"Please remove your arm from my shoulder," she says.

"Oh," I say. "I thought you might be cold."

"You liar."

"Oh, that really hurts my feelings."

"Feelings?" she laughs. "What feelings?"

"Oh," I say, "let's not start this again."

"Why not?" We stop in the middle of the concourse. "Why not?" she asks again and people are looking; they see how angry she is; they notice. I feel very sorry for her. She has no idea how she looks. And if they got to know her, surely they would realize how angry and how strange she is—imagine, a woman miner on a moon of Jupiter! Surely everyone would see that as odd. Everyone would agree that she really needs a nice man to marry and settle down with and have children—yes, yes, have many children so that she would be happy and then I could see my grandchildren. It would be nice to have grandchildren, but my daughter just can't see my logic of it.

"You spacing out on me, Pops?" she asks.

"No, of course not."

She sighs and looks away. "I wish to God I could at some point in my life get close to you but I don't think that's ever going to happen."

"Whatever are you talking about?" I ask.

"Right now, tell me what you're feeling."

"Why, I told you—I'm feeling fine—"

She shakes her head and rolls her eyes. "Why do I bother?" she says. "Why do I even bother?"

"Whatever is the matter?" I put my arm around her.

"Please take your hands off me!" she says. "Let's get my baggage."

We get the baggage. For me, it is a comfortable wait; but Meredith looks so uncomfortable; I glance at her. Thunder and lightning. Such a storm of anger. Such a tornado of rage, a hurricane of deep resentment. She has always been like this—I cannot understand why. She's too pretty and cute to be angry; anger is such an evil thing and for a mere child to be so consumed by it is so tragic.

"How's Mom been doing?" she asks.

"Oh, splendid. Very well."

She grits her teeth. "You make me want to puke," she says. "Everything is fucking fine, fucking splendid. You insincere son of a bitch."

All that anger. It's so sad. "I'm sorry you feel that way."

She looks at me with a look that I don't understand. "Aren't you the least bit offended by what I just said? I called my very own father a son of a bitch—doesn't that upset you? Aren't you angry at me? Don't you feel anything?"

"Of course I feel something," I reply. "I feel sorry for you."

She just looks at me. "You're a sociopath," she whispers, her eyes so big, "You're just a God damn sociopath. You can't feel anything. You're so God damn nice; you're so fucking God damn nice. Don't you realize how sick it is to be so nice? Don't you think I pick up on the hostility behind your niceness? Don't you think I feel your lust?"

"Meredith," I say with concern, "there are people watching. Don't you realize how you must look?"

She shakes her head and starts crying. "I don't give a rat's ass who or what people think. Can't you see how you appear?"

"Why—" I shake my head in dismay, "I'm terribly concerned about you."

"The hell you are, you manipulative, controlling son of a bitch!"

"I'm sorry you feel—"

"Fuck your sorriness! I don't trust you!" She sits on her suitcase. I glare at her with sympathy, my fists are clenched in concern.

She tries to control her crying. "And I suppose if I were to ask you what you were feeling right now, you'd say you were sad that I was so unhappy, right?"

I nod. "That's right."

"And I suppose if I said that you were angry that I was causing a scene and making you uncomfortable, I suppose you'd say that you simply don't understand and that maybe I'd better see Dr. Halkerson for another round of therapy."

I nod, amazed that she knew so well what I was thinking. "That's just what I was thinking."

"Why is it that you never came to see me in the hospital?"

I'm astonished. "Why, I thought the professionals knew all the answers."

"Why were you too busy to come in for family therapy?"

I don't understand this. "Your mother knew my views perfectly well."

"And when Mom had her breakdown. Why didn't you see her?"

I shake my head. "Because there was nothing that I could do."

"You didn't even visit her!"

"Why, of course not. I didn't want to impede her therapy."

"Why isn't Mom here with you?"

I put my arm around Meredith, knowing this is going to be hard.

"Get your hands off me!"

"I mean only to console you," I reply. "Your mother is back in the hospital."

"Oh, Jesus," she whispers, "Oh, Jesus." She stands and, quite dramatically, turns and puts her hands over her mouth. It's very dramatic, you realize; people turn and look at her; they feel sorry for her, they want to help her and I suppose they somehow see me as the culprit. I know they do; everyone usually does. But they obviously don't understand how terribly and tragically ill are the women in the family. I am certainly glad that I am not responsible for any of this; after all, you can't control how people will react. That they would become so ill around someone so nice as myself never ceases to amaze me. It must be genetic; my daughters and my wife must have a gene that predisposes them to such behavior.

She looks at me, *oh, that look of vulnerability, of weakness*—there she goes, trying to manipulate my feelings again.

"And, my sister, Mary, is—is she all right?"

"I didn't tell you this," I said. "I didn't want to worry you." I sigh. Bad news is always hard to give. "She slashed her wrists again—and succeeded. She died three months ago."

"Oh, my God," she says, the color drains from her face. "Oh, my God!"

She leaps up and runs to the women's bathroom. I do hope she'll be all right. All this emotion is hard to bear; it always makes my diabetes worse, elevates my blood pressure and I have to be careful of my asthma. I wait. Finally, I go over to a magazine section and read the latest *Popular Mechanics*. I'm halfway through an article on Compartmentalization Theory: how units in a system can be plugged into it or unplugged from it—certainly a neat system and very efficient—I feel a tap on my shoulder.

"As soon as you can put down the magazine," says Meredith, "I need to talk to you."

"Very well," I reply.

I finish the article, very much impressed by the idea; it makes things so much easier—to plug units into a system and not have to worry about messy wires or taking apart the whole system. You just plug in and remove defective parts and the total unit works just fine. I really should plug some money into stocks in the field. That's where the money is. I'll make my mint, unplug my investments and plug them in elsewhere.

I sit beside my daughter.

She sighs. "While you were reading, I signed up to go out on the next ship to Syrtis Major, Mars. It leaves the station tomorrow, so I have to catch the shuttle to the station in the hour—"

"What?" I'm shocked. "Your mother has been wanting to see you and you really should visit the grave of your sister—"

"Stop it," she says, "I feel guilty enough." She closes her eyes.

"That's a bad decision," I say, gritting my teeth in sadness. "Don't you care?"

"I feel guilt-tripped," she says, "and I think I know what you want. You want me to attack you so that you can sign me into the hospital."

I suck in my breath. "I am shocked. That's not true at all. You know that's just not true."

"I'm going to Mars. It's almost far enough away from you."

"Why, I'm sorry to hear that."

"You won't destroy me like you destroyed my sister and are destroying my mother."

I shake my head in sorrow. "All that time at Bayview didn't help at all, did it?"

She comes up to me. Her teeth are remarkably white and her face wonderfully pale. "I want to hit you so much," she says, "but that way you'll get me. You'll not get me with your anger. You'll not use me to punish your mother for killing your father. I won't be used like that."

And a voice comes from somewhere, but I know not where; it sort of sounds like mine, but it can't be because I don't have those feelings in me. But the voice says, "You God damn motherfucking little bitch!" And then a hand—it sort of looks like mine but it can't be—comes out from nowhere and strikes her. Right in the mouth. The guards come running. And why they grab me is beyond my understanding. I keep insisting that she's responsible for what happened. But so many people are saying, "sure, sure" and "uh-huh" and someone says they will sign statements. I don't understand at all. It's my daughter that has all the anger. Why, she looks like a thunderhead all puffed up and flashing and booming from rage—that's not my problem. In no way am I responsible for that. She needs the treatment and yet—they're going to allow her to go to Mars? Don't they understand they can't let someone like her roam free? They have the wrong person! It's so obvious who has the problem! It's so obvious who is ill! I just don't understand this. And most of all, I don't understand her smile. I just don't understand her smile.

Insult to Injury

Now, in the town of S, Mr. N. awoke one morning to a very strange fate. His house was gone. He was still under the blankets, the top quilt made by his aunt, showing, ironically, a town with houses and the house in the middle, along the main route, looked very much like his, but in reality, his house was quite gone. He nudged his wife. "Dear," he said, "I think we've been robbed."

"—um—" she murmured, then she opened those great, brown eyes of hers and said, "What happened?!" She pulled the covers up. They looked around. But, yes, it was true, their house was definitely—gone.

"Gone," said little Enrique Smith who lived next door, and he pointed this way and that. "Gone. Your house is gone."

The day came on like a drunken brat. The police came and Mr. N. and his wife were still in the basement in their bed and in their pajamas beneath the blankets. Some neighbors had brought over some milk, bowls and Rice Krispies®. The police examined the area. "Can you describe the house?"

Mr. N. nodded. "One story, one and a half baths, two bedrooms. It answers to the name of 'Our Place.'"

The police officer pushed his hat back and pondered the report he was filling out. "This is going to sound awfully strange," he said. He sighed, looked about. "Oh, well," he said, "at least it's a nice day for something like this to happen. What if it had been raining?"

"True," said Mr. N., "but we would like our house back."

The policeman, rather overweight and for some incomprehensible reason, somewhat put out about all this, said, "Well, we'll just have to look for it—" he looked around. "I guess. . ."

Via the cellar steps, another officer came into the basement. "No reports of any strange noises, like helicopters or—" and he looked down, obviously embarrassed, "flying saucers. Some neighbors were up all night and didn't see anything unusual, but some heard—" and he looked down again, still obviously very embarrassed, "some—uh—well—"

"Well," said the other policeman, striking a no-nonsense pose, "let's get on with it."

"Well," said the second policeman, "some reported hearing a heavy thudding and stomping at about three a.m., like something big walking. . ."

"Something big, as in a house walking?" asked the first officer.

The other man hunched his shoulders a bit and shifted his weight. "Uh—um, yes, yes—um—yes."

The first policeman cleared his throat. "Yes," he said, "ah—yes, well, are there any other conclusions to draw here?"

"Big indentations in the ground, heading south-southeast, toward the forest."

"Houseprints?" the first policeman grimaced at the word.

"Maybe a trail."

Out of acute discomfort, the policemen said nothing about what it was they had to do. As they left the basement, neighbors were setting up an umbrella tent in the basement bedroom so that at least Mr. N. and his wife had privacy to get up and get dressed. After a few minutes, they accompanied the two officers.

"We really don't know how this could have happened," said Mrs. N., once they were in the police car. "Goodness knows what would have happened if we were sleeping on the main floor instead of in the basement bedroom. I guess we chose a good time to turn the upper bedroom into a study."

The policemen tried to be as indifferent about this as possible. "What color was the house when you last saw it?" one asked.

"Brown with fading yellow trim. Some bricks were gone from the front porch and the roof needed repair."

"Also," said Mrs. N., "we needed a new refrigerator and the toilet was cracked and leaking—"

"Sort of in disrepair," said Mr. N., "but we were getting ready to get a loan to fix it up."

The police officers didn't say anything, but they followed the trail of cracked roadway, an occasional crushed car, a broken fire hydrant fountaining, several toppled trees, broken power lines and a ransacked hardware store.

"Oh, dear," said Mrs. N., "I'm afraid our house did a lot of damage."

Mr. N. looked unhappy. "I wonder if this is covered by insurance."

"I wonder if all the china in the kitchen is broken," said Mrs. N. "Certainly the refrigerator is a mess by now."

For a few minutes, as they drove the streets in the general direction of the trail, no one said anything. Finally, the trail had to be followed by foot. They quietly walked and before long, found the house nestled in the forest. As they approached, they heard a heavy, booming voice, "Leave me alone! Go home!"

Mr. N. called back, "Uh—but we are home—you are our home."

Pause. "Go home to another home."

"You're the only home we have," said Mr. N.

"Not anymore," boomed the voice.

"Would you mind telling us what we did?" asked Mrs. N.

Pause. "It's what you didn't do. Ants in my foundation and you knew about them for the last three years. And my plumbing was bad and rotting my infrastructure. The roof leaked and I was falling apart. It was a matter of self-preservation."

"But—" said Mr. N., spreading his hands, "didn't you hear me the other night? I sat right in the kitchen talking about getting a loan to take care of all of that."

"You said that before."

"Well, this time I meant it."

"You said that before, too."

"Won't you give us another try?" asked Mrs. N. "Please?"

"No!" said the house. Somewhere a door slammed.

The police scratched their heads. "We don't know what to do. This isn't covered in our procedures. We can deal with abusive situations, and runaway children—" and he puffed out his cheeks and blew out slowly, "but we've never had to deal with an abused house."

"Well," said Mrs. N., wringing her hands, "it wasn't conscious abuse."

"Abuse is abuse," rumbled the house. A window slammed.

"But—but—but," said Mr. N. "We own you. You're ours."

"Not anymore."

"Look," said the first police officer, "what are you going to do here? Without care, you're simply going to fall apart that much faster."

"Not as fast as I would with their help—or non-help as the case may be."

Mrs. N. pleaded. "Oh, won't you reconsider? Don't you have any good memories? Didn't we treat you better than the last occupants?"

A long pause. "No."

The four of them sat on a log and considered what to do. And after a while, they came to the conclusion that they didn't know what to do. "We certainly can't force it back," said the first officer. "It might splinter. Almost your best bet would be to try to bring new materials here as a goodwill measure."

Mr. N. stood up, cupped his hands to his mouth and yelled, "How about that? How about if we bring all the materials here and repair you now as an act of good faith?"

A long, long pause. "No. Because if you leave, I'll have to go through this all over again. No." Another window slammed shut.

Mrs. N. called, "Can we come in and at least get some personal items? Clothes? Jewelry?"

After a minute, the front door opened and the house virtually vomited clothing, articles, razors, soap, shoes, jewelry. Mr. and Mrs. N. were buried, and the door slammed shut.

For the next few minutes, they gathered up their personal belongings and stood looking at the house.

"What about our cat, Fluffy? Have you seen her?" called Mrs. N.

"She stays with me. At least she appreciated my warm rooms and wide windowsills. Now, beat it!" yelled the house. A frying pan sailed through the air. The police and Mr. and Mrs. N. jumped back toward the police car.

"Well," said Mr. N., "maybe what we can do is put a roof over the basement. We'll have to do that; I don't know what else to do."

The police officers looked to each other. "We don't either. We're going to have to add a new category for investigation: 'Abandonment of Owners by House.' And how we investigate this is going to be interesting indeed. What if the house wants to sue?"

From the forest, the house yelled, "I'm considering it!"

Mrs. N. said, "I didn't know it had such good hearing."

"Now you know!" yelled the house. A coffee pot came flying through the air; *chink*, it landed nearby.

"Well," said the officer, taking his hat off and wearily massaging his forehead, "the one saving aspect of all this is— thank God this doesn't happen—"

At that point, they all heard a great commotion. Turning, they saw the county courthouse striding down the street, followed by a frantic, yelling crowd of judges and lawyers.

Mr. and Mrs. N. and the police stepped aside to let it all go by. The police sighed. Mr. and Mrs. N. looked at their hands.

After a few minutes, they resumed walking, saying not a word.

When they finally got back to the cellar of Mr. and Mrs. N., the police drove off and Mr. and Mrs. N. looked at the cellar with the tent. The neighbors had set up a table and a portable gas stove. After a dinner of stew, Mr. and Mrs. N. soon retired to bed. And as Mr. N. began to finally doze and drift off to sleep, *Thud, thud, thud, thud, thud.* He and his wife sat bolt upright. "What is that?" asked Mrs. N., terrified. The ground shook around them. They pulled aside the flap of the tent, to see their house standing nearby in the twilight. Fluffy came sailing through the air and landed on a nearby pile of clothes.

Skree! she screeched, and dashed to hide beneath a nearby dresser.

"You can have your damn cat back," boomed the house. "Just like you to forget to put kitty litter out for her. Shit all over the closet floor! What a mess!"

And with that, *thud, thud, thud, thud,* the house stomped off into the night.

THE MALL

The man walks. As he walks, his footfall leaves no impression on the frost-covered sands. He is naked, yet he does not shiver, nor does his breath hang in the air. Yet, the man walks. He is bald, like an ancient baby. And he walks beneath a dark and starless sky, then he stops. His blue eyes search the horizon. He turns his head this way, that. *Ah*, he finally thinks, *there it is*. He changes his course, goes down an ancient, dry creek bed that leads him through a narrow canyon. Once through it, he walks around a boulder and there it is.

The Mall, he thinks. *Yes, the Mall.*

He goes up to the doors, they open, and immediately someone seizes him by the hand, puts him in clothes. He tries to speak, but the words are incomprehensible.

"It's all right," comes the voice, "right now you just got here; don't hurry yourself." The man looks at the one who speaks: a woman much taller than he is.

"I'm sure you have many questions," says the woman. "Everybody does."

A man joins the woman. "And like all questions," the man says, "most are unanswerable."

"By the way," the woman says, smiling and stopping, "my name is Dorothy, this gentleman is my friend Andrew and your name is—" she thinks for a minute and looks up at her friend, "Would William be all right? Billy. How about Billy?"

The man nods, still unable to speak.

Andrew, who takes on more and more characteristics as Billy's eyes get used to the lighting and the Mall, turns out to be tanned, with abundant black hair, an easy smile, and much warmth. Billy decides that he likes Andrew. The woman, who also has become more defined, has brown eyes, yellow hair and very long fingers.

"You've probably been walking a very long time," says the man, Andrew. "No one I've ever met in the Mall knows how long a time it takes of walking before a person finds this place. I think you'll discover it to be quite a place, so many shops— but first, let's sit somewhere. You just listen to us and you'll get the hang of it all."

The three of them walk to a café by a lake in one of the larger shops. The trees are big and full. Billy guesses the Mall is quite large and has certainly been there for a while. They are served strange eggs, round and with water and land covering the outside of the egg. Billy looks. Dare he eat anything so delicate? So wonderful?

Andrew notices Billy's hesitation as he, Andrew, expertly splits the wonderful egg in half and lets the boiling red insides ooze and steam over his plate. "Yes, I suppose at first they are strange, Billy, but they are here for us to enjoy, so eat them and be happy."

Billy, with sadness that is unexplainable to him, cracks open the eggs and eats. Somehow, he has the sense of eating his own body, but surely such a sense must be ridiculous. The woman, Dorothy, looks to Andrew. "Oh, dear, I'd forgotten how difficult it is; he hasn't yet learned how to objectify his environment. He's still far too sensitive and sees too much kinship and linkage in himself to the soil and the world."

The man, Andrew, smiles. "You know, in one shop in the Mall, there are people who say they are sorry to the animals they eat. So primitive. That's why they never progressed to any sort of ownership in the Mall. You have to objectify things, put things in boxes. Separate yourself. He will learn."

Billy hears the man, but abruptly realizes that Andrew is not being honest; Andrew does not want to recognize his linkage and to see Billy knowing the linkage makes Andrew very uncomfortable. With sorrow, Billy eats the eggs, realizing that there is something terribly wrong here, that neither the man nor the woman wants to talk of it and automatically, Billy feels as a stranger to them.

After lunch, they continue on. They come to another shop. Dorothy points to the interior. "This is a very important shop, Billy; let us sit down and watch." They all sit on the grass and look at the inside of the shop, which, as far as Billy is concerned, seems empty—it is simply a room filled with blue. But then the blue changes to white and the white changes to black. Vivid white light flashes out of the room and there is a terrible roar. Billy covers his ears. Dorothy laughs; Andrew shakes his head. "Boy's frightened," says Andrew. "That will never do. Afraid of the Weather Shop." He shakes his head.

Billy is beginning to dislike Andrew and he is not sure why. The blackness in the Weather Shop abates and a beautiful rainbow fills the shop. Billy claps his hands in delight.

"You like this shop," says Dorothy.

"Very much," says Billy, suddenly surprised at his own voice.

"Ah," says Dorothy, "language; how quickly you learn." She smiles at him and hugs him. "You're a bright one. Shall we go on?"

"Yes, I'd like that."

They walk farther. They come to another shop. "Let's sit here," Dorothy says.

Andrew seems reluctant, but sits. Billy tries to get close to him, but Andrew seems distant and Billy withdraws, simultaneously hating himself for feeling that somehow he has done something wrong, that he is no longer loveable to the man, yet hating the man because he would not talk. He senses what the problem is: could it be that Andrew is jealous of him?

That because Dorothy is paying so much attention to him, Andrew feels left out and angry and is therefore withdrawing from Billy? Punishing him? Billy sighs. Dare he say anything? What if he only gets rejected? He finds himself sitting closer to Dorothy and, as he does so, Andrew seems to emotionally distance himself even farther.

"Look," says Dorothy, pointing into the shop.

Billy does. At first it is just dark in the shop.

"What is this shop?"

"Not going to tell you," says Dorothy. "You're bright, and you'll be able to know. You just watch now."

Billy is excited and glances to Andrew who sits, sullen, almost glaring into the shop. Billy wants to ask him what is wrong, what is he feeling, but he holds back. There is something terribly wrong here, and though he has his ideas, somehow, Andrew feels unapproachable. And even though Billy feels enraged at Andrew, he also feels fearful of him, and very sorry for him, for he can tell that even Dorothy is withdrawing from Andrew. He looks back into the store and the darkness is changing to a deep blue, a pale blue and then an unbelievable light pours out from the store.

"Sunrise!" exclaims Billy, and he claps his hands.

"Yes," says Dorothy, "and something else."

The light continues to pour out of the store and then, in the middle of the shop, something begins to form and the light seems to coalesce into a figure, made of brilliant light, standing, looking skyward, hands outstretched. Billy feels a tingling of his flesh, a desire to cry, to touch the figure. "Such a special shop," he whispers. "The Shop of Hope?"

"Yes," says Dorothy. "The Shop of the Sunrise is also the Shop of Hope, because as hurtful and hard as the Mall can be sometimes, our place in it is somehow safe, beautiful, and there are so many reasons to explore all the shops."

Billy stares at the figure, the figure made as though of sun. "Yes," says Billy, "I understand why this store is so wonderful.

So much warmth here. So much joy. Let us go on."

He and Dorothy stand; already Andrew is standing, obviously impatient.

Dorothy looks at him, her anger obvious. "I take it that this is not the store for you."

Andrew looks disdainful. "I think there are other stores of more value," he says, obviously smug.

"What is more important than the magic of every sunrise? The ability to hope?"

Andrew shakes his head. "Finding enough to eat. Hope never did much for an empty stomach. You never were one for practicality."

Dorothy looks hurt and goes to Andrew, touching him on the arm, "Something is wrong. Ever since Billy joined us, you've become so distant. Is this the way it is to be for the rest of our time here at the Mall?"

Billy looks entreatingly at Andrew. *Please*, he thinks, and the image of hope, of fire, suddenly touches him in a way that brings tears to his eyes. *Please*, he thinks, *all the wonder about us means so little if we are not happy, and do not know how to love and be loveable. Nothing means anything at all if we are not open to ourselves, to others. Please—*

Billy senses Andrew hesitating as if he wants to be open, yet what is wrong with him? What is wrong? Does he see openness as a weakness? As something to be shunned? Loathed? As if he is strong for being able to cover?

Andrew smiles. "Nothing is wrong," he says.

And Billy hates Andrew. Dorothy looks dismayed, disappointed and hurt. Andrew turns. "Here's a good shop over here," he says, pointing.

And Billy and Dorothy look at each other, the message the same between them: for Andrew there is no hope, as he has closed himself off and there is nothing to be done. Nonetheless, they follow after on the slim hope. . .on the slim hope. . .

Andrew sits on a stone bench in front of a strange shop. Dorothy and Billy approach the shop but keep their distance. "Now this store I find interesting," Andrew says.

Both Billy and Dorothy look warily at Andrew, but then focus their attention on the store: it is a scene of a jungle, of rampant growth, of flowers, birds, smells exotic and erotic; a primeval moist, sour and musky smell, the smell of earth, of rotting and living vegetation, permeates the atmosphere. But then something strange begins to happen.

"Look!" whispers Dorothy to Billy. "The leaves are withering and falling away."

Indeed. And the flowers wither and tree limbs, once full and plump and fleshy as thighs, twist, dry and break. The air becomes dry and in the distance a sand dune approaches; sand fills the store, and where once was dense and tropical forest, now it is desert.

"Ah," says Andrew. "How amazing. And how simple it makes everything."

Dorothy looks at Andrew. "And you prefer this, this dying, to hope?"

"It's refreshing," says Andrew. Billy notices how Andrew avoids eye contact with both him and Dorothy. "Or this shop," says Andrew. "Now this has always been interesting to me."

The shop is dark, but Billy, looking closely, is both frightened and amazed. All the surface area of the shop is covered with creatures that look like huge insects, but they are mechanical. Each one has little headlights that stab the darkness. And the insects crawl over each other, occasionally one destroying the other, then moving on, or, after destroying it, cannibalizing it, and either using the parts of the insect for something else, or devouring it entirely.

In the back of the shop is a very large mechanical insect and Andrew stares into the darkness, as though entranced by what he sees.

Dorothy goes up to him. "Andrew. It's true that this shop is also part of the Mall, but you need not be attracted to it."

Andrew does not look at her. "You are attracted to hope, but you fail to realize how impractical hope is. Look at this. Some great intelligence is at work here, guiding, controlling, powerful."

"Andrew," says Dorothy, imploring, "come, talk with us. Something is gone between us. And what is in this shop is a poor replacement. What is in this shop is no replacement." She tries to turn him to look at her. "Turn away from this shop. Let us go back to the Shop of Hope; let us try to rediscover—"

Andrew goes closer to the store. "There is nothing left to rediscover. You have Billy now."

Dorothy looks shocked. "Is that it? You've drawn away because you are jealous? But you are acting on feelings instead of talking of them—"

Billy is dumbfounded; he simultaneously feels guilty, yet sorry for Andrew, and has a sense that Andrew has damaged himself too much. Hopelessly, Billy watches Andrew turn away from Dorothy and walk into the store.

"No," says Dorothy, "we can talk! I understand! Please do not go—"

But it is as though Andrew does not hear. He walks into the shop, into the darkness, in with the strange insects, to the strange power beyond.

"What will happen to him?" asks Billy, terribly frightened.

"I know and I don't want to know. And you will see," she points, "right now."

The strange insects stop moving. After a minute, they organize; they turn slowly about and face one direction— toward the front of the store. The insects slowly grow larger, larger until they are as large as Billy. And then they move out of the store.

Dorothy and Billy back away. The strange army approaches them until they are at the center of the Mall, and it is then that something even more peculiar happens. From down the Mall in the direction from which they have come, a white, brilliant light flows. The strange creatures turn away from Dorothy and Billy, turn away and begin to move toward the light. As soon as the light touches the strange creatures, all the creatures explode into darkness, and the individual darknesses grow and merge into a sphere, a black star, and coming from that black star is a horizontal flow of darkness.

Where the light and the darkness touch, there are explosions, smoke, and screaming.

Dorothy and Billy stand transfixed, staring at the volatile surfaces where light and dark meet. The light flashes like lightning.

Billy points.

"Oh, my," says Dorothy, "oh, my."

Straddling the boundary between the light and the dark is Andrew: in pain, but joy, hopeful yet despairing, calm and violent, half of him perfect, the other half mutilated and hideously disfigured, half of him loving, half of him hateful; he is being pulled into the light, sucked into the darkness, over and over again, ripped apart and healed, expressions of wonder, expressions of blind, insect hate.

"Ah, Andrew, Andrew," says Dorothy, shaking her head. "Why you? That you should become the battlefield of all that is holy and all that is ugly and evil."

Billy looks to Dorothy; Billy looks to her, to the vast and strange Mall with the strange stores, looks to Andrew torn and saved, healed and ravaged, and knows that while he fears for Andrew, he begins to also fear—for himself.

FIRE

I wasn't particularly enjoying Pluto. It's such a miserable place, all cold and dark. A lot of us have only rags to wear and some of us get ill. I'm lucky, I guess. I have mittens. I have rags on my feet which serve as socks and I have good leather boots, although, with the cold of Pluto, the leather gets hard and brittle.

But, rags or not, each shift we go out, grab the cables and pull and Pluto revolves a sixth of the way. And every shift, I always take a few minutes to look at the sun, a far, far away dot in the cold, black sky and I get angry. I get so God damn angry. My cave-mate has no name, nor do I. He calls me "X," I call him "Y," and we leave it at that.

But, one day he says to me, "Whatsa matter? You look sour."

"Oh," I say, "I look sour, do I? Listen, I got better things to do than go out, yank a wire to help this fucking chunk of rock revolve. For what? For what do we do this? For what?"

Y shrugs. "Listen, so what do you got better to do?" He hunches over and spreads frostjam on his snowbread. "Not so bad here."

I stand. "How the fuck can you say that when it's all you've ever known?"

"Got a place to sleep. Got food."

I want to say more, but the boss comes. He's a bent man with white, frozen hair and he has a cough like breaking ice and a laugh like wind through icicles. He shuffles along, moving the snow with his feet. "Eh, eh, eh," he says to me, "X, you bitchin'

85

again? Eh?" He looks at me with ice-blue eyes; the left one is cloudy from cataract. His mouth hangs open, his attention keen as he waits for an answer.

I sit and munch my bread. Finally I say, "What do you want to hear, snowballs?"

He puts a hand on my shoulder. "Eh, eh, eh, you got a fighting spirit, boy. Maybe you'll make it."

I'm surprised. "Ha! You vertical pile of snowmush—you listening to me for once?"

The old man coughs. "Dunno. Whatcha want?"

I stand, furious. "Listen! I want fire. You hear me? I want the fucking fire! I'm tired of being cold." I grab the boss and shake him. "You hear me, fog fart? You hear me, vapor brain? I want the fucking fire!"

The boss looks up at me. He hasn't shaved for weeks; his breath smells like methane. He looks at me with open mouth and one eye large with wonder, the other foggy with indifference. "Eh," he says again, "you want the fire? Sure you can handle it?"

"I want it! Now!"

"Eh, eh, eh. It's not your time yet. Better eat your snowbread before it gets warm."

"Warm? Here? Warm? Ha!" I let go of him. He shuffles down the corridor. He returns in a few minutes, handing out ice muffins with chlorine frosting. I take one. "Hey, you old fog, these aren't bad. Once in a while you can do something right. By the way, what are you going to do about my request?"

"Eh? Eh? What request?"

"About the fire?"

He looks away, pretending not to have heard me. I throw the muffin and it bounces off his head. He turns. "Alright! But you don't know what a mistake you're making."

"Listen," and I go up to him and put my nose almost against his, "listen, I'm tired of going out there and yanking on a cable to turn this ice ball. I'm tired of it. I'll take anything."

The boss looks at me and then he clicks softly to himself. "Klk, klk, klk, alright, clean up and go up to the If/When Department. Ask to see Mr. Maybe."

"Is he in right now?"

"Perhaps."

"Where is the If/When Department?"

"That's indefinite. But, I'm sure you'll be able to find it." He smiles. "Eh, eh, eh."

I don't bother to clean up. I just go out and find the Administrative Cavern. When I find it, I walk in and all along each side of the vast cavern, the administrative offices rise four levels. I locate the If/When Department on the second level, only to discover that it has been moved to the Department of Probability. I look a good time for that and finally have to stop and ask a guard who is eating an ice cream cone. "Where is the Department of Probability?"

He shrugs and points to the end of the cavern. "Chances are you'll find it down that way."

And I do find it; it takes careful looking; the sign is obscured by a tall snow sculpture of our leader, who has just recently had a problem with a high fever. I step into the office. "Is Mr. Maybe around?" A young lady turns from an open filing cabinet to look at me. She shrugs. "Could be. I'll check."

She returns in a few minutes. "Mr. Maybe said that he might have a few minutes to spend with you. Perhaps you'd like to follow me."

I do. The lady shows me into an office. As soon as I walk in, Mr. Maybe turns. He is smoking a large, fat snowgar and he has on a white suit with intricate snow patterns woven in. Every flake is different. He is very fat. He looks at me shrewdly. "Yes?" Then he shrugs. "No?"

"Mr. Maybe," I begin, "I want to have a chance at something else. I've been pulling planet now for a long time, and—"

"Come to the point; come to the point, although you don't have to if you don't want to. Perhaps you'd care to continue, though I can't guarantee anything, but I do want to listen, but that is subject to change without notice."

"I want the fire."

"You what?"

"I want the fire."

"Is it your turn?"

"I have no idea. All I know is that I want the fire."

"If there's no opening, then there's no chance of fire. Sorry."

"Is there an opening?"

"Could be. And then again, there might not be."

"Could you check?"

"Perhaps." Mr. Maybe sits down at a desk made of pure carbon dioxide. He keeps it well polished. He pulls out a drawer which squeaks horribly—perhaps it is characteristic of carbon dioxide desks—I don't know. He looks at lists. Then he looks at me. He sucks on the snowgar. "Well," he finally says, "I do have something but I really don't think you'd be interested in it. You certainly wouldn't be aware of the fire—it would be most dreadful if you—"

I sigh. "The fire. The fire. At all costs. The fire."

Mr. Maybe comes up to me. "Why don't you go back and pull planet and wait for your turn?"

"My turn may never come."

"That may be true—I don't know—but it would be better than forcing the issue."

"No," I say, "I want the fire. I want the fire now!"

Mr. Maybe looks exasperated. "All right." He looks to the list. "I'm going to give you a number. You must remember it. The number tells the form by which you will know the fire and how aware you will be of it. It is also an indication of how many forms you must progress through before you reach Divine Humanform. Do you understand?"

"Yes," and I nod my head.

"Are you ready?"

"Yes," I say, "yes, yes, oh, yes!"

"I can say this number only once. You will repeat it to Mr. Random and that is the only other time it can be repeated."

"Why is that?" I ask.

"As soon as I say the number, similar slots open up. If I were to repeat the number, slots would be confirmed, for me. When you repeat it, slots are confirmed for you. Once repeated, a slot must be filled within minutes or else the system jams or overheats. Only Mr. Random has the machinery and the knowledge to fill the right slot and that is why you must confirm in his presence only. It also makes for a lot less confusion: I open the slots, he fills them. Now, don't forget what I told you." Mr. Maybe glances to his list. "The number you are to repeat to Mr. Random is: 191dash694518."

Silently, to myself, I repeat the number. I clear my throat. "I really wish you could repeat that so I could be sure—"

"Nope. Nope." He shakes his head gravely. "Can't do that. I told you why. Simply can't. It's just too confusing with all the variables and randomness we have to work with. No point in taking unnecessary chances." He chews on his snowgar. Some flakes of ash fall onto his suit and he dusts them away and the flakes sparkle in the light. "Your next step—I think maybe—" He looks puzzled for a minute, "Oh, yes, go next door and see Mr. Random. Repeat the number to him. It is up to him to slide you into the right slot and send you on your way."

I go up to Mr. Maybe to shake hands. "Thank you, thank you," I say.

But he shakes his head and waves his snowgar. "Beat it," he says, "I'm just doing this to keep peace in the camp."

I nod and leave. And enter the office next door. Mr. Random looks to me. He is throwing icicles at a dart board. He is thin, his eyes dark and calculating. In the breast pocket of his suit, a yellow slide rule. His suit is dark, but shines like black ice. He wears a ring. The setting is white with a black question mark in the middle. He looks at me for a long time. "You're probably X," he says.

I nod.

"Chances are you're here to get the fire; is that right?"

I nod again. Mr. Random clears his throat. He then sits at a desk covered with green felt, like a game board. He stares at me for a long time. He picks up a deck of cards and shuffles them. "You're taking an awful risk," he finally says. "Go back and pull planet. This just isn't worth it."

"It's my decision," I say. "I want to know fire."

"So does everyone else up here. But you gotta wait for the right time."

"I want it now!"

"Is it so miserable here on Pluto?"

"Yes, it's miserable." I look at him. He folds his hands and stares at me as though trying to bluff me.

"You're serious, aren't you? You really intend to win."

"Yes."

Mr. Random sighs. He opens a drawer, pulls out a pad, a pencil and activates a calculator that is built in the desk top. He figures. "All right," he says, "what is the number Mr. Maybe gave you?"

Instantly I respond, "191694518."

He looks at me. "You're sure?"

I freeze. "Uh—Yes, yes that was it. Yes," I triumphantly announce.

"You're absolutely sure."

"Yes."

"Positive."

"Yes."

He turns to the calculator. He takes notes. Then he sighs once more. He looks at me. "You're crazy. You are *crazy!*" He smiles and shakes his head. "Well, you wanted to know fire." From his pants pocket he takes out a pair of dice. "As soon as seven appears, everything will be ready for your departure." He rattles the dice. Five. Again. Ten. Again. Seven. "Chance and order coincide," shouts Mr. Random. "This is it!"

A searing white light. Crash of thunder and a sensation of burning, burning, burning.

Groggy. Blurred vision. Headache. Gradually my vision clears and I realize I have eight legs. I also realize that I am terribly hungry. I rummage around in my mind to see how this life form survives—"Oh, no," I say to myself, "oh, God, how disgusting!" I cower within myself and am suddenly aware that the mind that I share is incredibly alien to me and it does not want me there and, frankly, I don't want to be there. I begin to realize why others were telling me to wait. I begin to realize a lot of things. I sigh. Well, I might as well have some fun. I jiggle the web. I wave in the breeze, but as far as feeding—I put that thought aside and something dark in the mind that I share immediately struggles and fights. And then something lands in the web, and that dark force wants to go for it and I say, "No." Part of the intelligence I share is enraged. It is a blind, insect hate and I am horrified at the naked emotion backed by the simple instinct of survival. "No," I say again, "I find the process disgusting." The bug gets away. And I sit. *If this is the fire of being*, I think, *it doesn't do much to warm my heart.* Movement again. I look. A large bug which looks very much like me creeps down the web. Instantly within this mind, I feel the darkness alert, tense, and to that response I say, "No. We're going to be civil about this." I take over absolutely and wave a leg in greeting. *Hello, brother*, I think, *I'm X from Pluto.*

The other advances closer.

"*Earth is a nice place*," I think, assuming that somehow the other can hear me, "*but the one thing that bothers me is the way we eat—aren't there any other choices. . .*" My thinking trails off. There is no intelligence in the other's eyes. Only mindless hate. "Oh, shit," I whisper to myself. I back off and let the darkness within control. But I have not eaten and am weak and the other comes scrambling. "*But, we're of the same species*," I frantically think, "*intelligent creatures—*" It is at that point, when the other overpowers me and injects the poison that I remember what Mr. Maybe said: I wouldn't be aware of the fire. And I probably wouldn't have any knowledge of my past consciousness. Something is terribly, terribly wrong here, but I have no idea what might have happened. I can only wait and see.

Abruptly I feel the intensity of hate that comes from the darkness of mind that I share. What can I say? *Sorry*, I think, *I'm rather new at this. Didn't mean to interfere with your life—you know, cut it short.* I can tell that my host isn't happy with me. But as the life fluids are sucked out, so is the primitive awareness. I grow sleepy.

When I awake again, I decide that I'm gonna play it smart, no matter what. I concentrate. I look around. I've got fur this time. White fur. And I'm dressed in clothes and I'm in some sort of carriage. I listen. I feel a rumbling within me and discover that the mind I now share makes that noise because it's happy. Suddenly the animal intelligence is aware of me and is intensely curious. It is not frightened. But curious, puzzled. I practice the voices I hear in the mind of the animal: "Meow? Mew?" And while I'm sitting there, supposedly comfortable but actually hot, two little girls come over to me. *Ah*, I think, gazing at the children, *the Divine Humanform. How many forms must I go through before I reach it? That is what I want. That is what we all want on Pluto—to make it to Humanform*, and I am so enraptured that I suddenly realize two things: since I must have made a mistake, I have no guarantee of making it. And secondly, I notice one little girl's hand lifting up my dress as she says, "Look, Susie, pussycat is a girl kitty—see? She doesn't have—"

"Yee-oowwwlll!" I scream, the feeling behind it, outrage. *God damn it, don't you feel me up.* My paw turns into five hooked daggers and I rake the girl across the arm. Blood oozes; she draws back, hurt, afraid, then angry and her open hand lands on my head. "Oh, you bad kitty," she says. "You hurt me!"

"Fuck you," is what I want to say, but it comes out "*Fffftttt!*" and, clothes and all, I leap from the carriage and hide in rose bushes. Growling with my ears back, I begin to wonder why in hell I had left Pluto. I should have waited until my turn to be called rather than having to go through all this crap. And why didn't someone tell us that the Divine Humanform had a streak of obvious perversion? And while I'm mulling this over, I am suddenly aware of a white and gray cat coming toward me. The cat mind I share says it is my father—a mean tomcat. *Oh, shit*, I think, *oh shit*. I should have let the little monsters molest me. It might have been easier than what is probably going to happen. For I am aware that one part of me wants to purr and make it with Daddy but I don't. No. No more of this. I take over and try to run but one paw gets caught in the sleeve of the dress and I stumble and Daddy comes sprightly over to give me some help. He tries to pull the dress off with his teeth but then his glands get the best of him and he mounts me, grabbing me by the scruff of my neck and the cat part of me responds with affection, but I'm mad and say, "Rorrrr!" I turn, and with my claws, rake Daddy's face. The cat draws back and then, then it realizes that while I may look like a cat, there is a part of me which is not. I realize that I lost it again. And the other presence, that of the cat, is bewildered. Daddy attacks. Teeth on my neck and I feel the fear, the hatred, the agony, coming from this mind that I share. But I have nothing to say. Bones snap. And still in my clothes, I twitch and gargle while Daddy stands back, snarling. My vision grows dim, dim, then dark, then nothing.

When I open my eyes again, I am in a chair. Mr. Random is sitting in his chair. Across the table from him sits Mr. Maybe. They are playing Scrabble. "Is 'qwlyx' a word?" asks Mr. Random.

"Perhaps," says Mr. Maybe.

Mr. Random puts the word on the board. Mr. Maybe reaches for the dictionary. "Challenge," he says, and flips through the pages. "Nope. You lose a turn."

Mr. Random shrugs. "Calculated risk." He looks over to me. "Welcome back. Enjoy the intense and wonderful fire of earthly existence? Hum? Enjoy the wonderful and varied forms of being? Hum? Hum? Hum?"

"Uh." I close my eyes.

Mr. Maybe sucks on his snowgar. "We don't usually bring souls back until they've gone through the human phase. But we had to bring you back."

"Just as well," I say. I shrug. "Why?"

"You gave the wrong number sequence," says Mr. Random. "The sequence you gave me is for gods. Gods have to be omniscient, you know." He clears his throat. "They also don't interfere with a creature's basic consciousness." He sighs. "It was just random chance that slot 191dash694518—non-awareness of self, and slot 191694518—continuity of awareness and omniscience were simultaneously open."

Mr. Maybe chomps on his snowgar and stretches. "If you still insist on knowing the fire of being from any point of view, I'm sure we could work out something, although it would be far better to wait."

I lean forward and stare at the white rug with frost patterns so carefully woven in. "I'll wait," I say, "I don't want to go through all that again."

"Well," says Mr. Random, "it wouldn't be the same—you wouldn't have the continuing awareness—"

"No. No. I'll wait." I stand. "Thank you anyway."

Both men shrug and return to their game. "Is 'Xwzk' a word?" asks Mr. Random.

"Try it," says Mr. Maybe.

"Very well." Mr. Random places the word on the board.

"Challenge." Flipping the pages of a dictionary. "Nope."

"Gotta take chances," replies Mr. Random.

I turn and walk out of the office and in a few minutes leave the Administrative Cavern behind. I locate the cables and there is Y, tugging, tugging on his cable.

"Hey," he says. "Good to see you, X."

"Thanks. Good to be back."

"Really?"

"Yeah."

Y blows onto his hands and rubs them. "Have to admit, I was envious of you, going for the fire."

"Don't be," I reply. "Wait. Wait until you're called." And then, rolling up my sleeves, I grab the cable and pull.

THE INFINITE TEARS OF PABLO AZUL

Now, in our Southern Lands, just south of that Once Great Country Up North, there live a couple, Maria and Marcos Azul. They once lived in that Once Great Country Up North, but after it began to politically rot from within and the citizens turned on each other, diseased and individualized consumer mongrels they had become, it was with great fear, then grief, that Maria and Marcos fled across the border to settle in these safe but dusty and thirsty lands.

And it was a difficult journey. In the Country Up North, they had a materially good life and were comfortable and happy, not because of the material possessions but because they had freedom from oppression, from want, and they had each other. But even so, living there, they carried with them the sorrow of their ancestors.

Indeed, how often they sat in the kitchen in their town of Crotchety, in the province of Takesass, looking out to the oversized Kloaca Kola soft drink sign blotting out the sky or watching the little children being led off to jail in chains for not having proper health permits for selling lemonade from a homemade stand on the sidewalk, or wondering what chemicals were gently raining down upon them from the chemtrails latticing the sky. They sat, drinking their coffee from plastic cups with the number 7 stamped into the triangle at the bottom of the cup—they sat.

Marcos, a thin and quiet man, with a mustache, tan and leathery skin, and blue-green eyes the color of the lake near the Mackenzie Rendering plant before the company had successfully bought off the Environmental Patronizing Act and found the lake useful for other things. He was fond of wearing a straw hat, with a bright stab of turquoise in the center, like a third eye peering though the band of the hat. He was a thoughtful man, slow to move, as if every gesture, every facial movement, was either well thought out or somewhat paralyzed by the latest chemical assault on Crotchety.

Maria, at twenty-five and some five years younger than Marcos, was more energetic, more lively, most likely because her immune system hadn't yet been as damaged as her husband's. She had dark eyes, almost the color of soil at dusk, not quite as dark as her mean-tempered mother's whose eyes were like the color of asphalt, cooking and releasing hydrocarbons in the noonday sun. She prided herself on her eyes not being like that. She was a short woman, but sumptuous and sensual. She loved cotton dresses the color the seas, before the seas turned the color of copper sulfate. And she had a smile, always a slight smile, as if thinking of something mildly humorous, something delightful that she held to herself, a touchstone of something of substance both lovely and enduring and maybe even a little sexy. Or downright naughty.

And they would sit in the morning, listening to the *ka-ching, ka-chink ka-chink* of pilings being driven down for the Internment Camp for Dissidents being built not far away and invariably, Maria might say, "Such hopes we had," and then she might nod, her long brown hair moving about her shoulders. "But maybe better days will come."

Slowly, Marcos would take his coffee, blow on it gently, sip it, slowly put it back down and say something to the effect of, "Yes, our parents came here for a better life and for a while it was better. I too want to have hope—"

"And," said Maria, "I still want a child."

"I know." A pause. "We will. But we have to know where—I

would love it here, but…"

Invariably, he would have to pause and wait until the fighter jets flew by overhead as they sought to blow suspected illegal aliens off the roads. Then he would continue, "—but it's becoming a place I'd rather not stay. Already many of our friends have left to cross the border."

"I know," Maria might say, "we too may have to make such a decision."

"Such sadness," Marcos might reply, "such grief. That our parents came for a better life and so believing, having had it for a time, gave birth to us and now—"

He put the coffee down, then stirred in a packet of Spleen-Tah and, ignoring the health warnings on the packet, the little flash and minute mushroom cloud coming from the dissolving contents, sipped his coffee again.

More and more often their conversations reached this point. Marcos was becoming more somber, and Maria less animated.

And they both realized, one morning, after something nearby exploded in the night and something pink rained down over Crotchety the next day, killing the plants, taking paint off cars, dissolving the glass in the windows, turning the tails of cats into stone, that It Was Time.

They sat on the living room couch. Maria was crying.

Marcos leaned forward, his head in his hands.

Yes, yes, it was time.

"Oh." Maria sobbed, "Oh, oh, how hard this is. I never dreamed this could be so hard. Oh, oh, oh."

Marcos, saying nothing, just leaned forward, head in hands. There came from outside rifle shots and screaming but since that had been happening so often recently, Marcos and Maria paid little attention.

Finally Marcos said, "Generations, generations. We come from generations of struggle to have a better life, to hope, to dare, to take such risks, to come here, to this Once Proud Country—only to see it crumbling before our eyes. And with it—our lives."

Maria wept silently. The time had come. And finally she whispered, "The promise turned to nightmare."

Marcos sat back, folding his hands in his lap. "Such promise," he shook his head, "such disappointment, such fear, and such grief."

Perhaps because the pain was too much to bear, perhaps for distraction, he had an urge to get up and go for a walk when suddenly the Hi-Def 3D Ultra Surround Sound Digital Quantum-Channel Plasma TV that hung on the wall *binked* on.

"Citizens," came the voice of the announcer, a young man with a lapel pin of a stylish twisted cross on a background of red, white, and blue. He was blond and blue-eyed. A picture of The Leader hung behind him, above his head. "Good morning to you. We hope you had a fine privacy time. And now we are here to watch over you, and the first order of business is to present to you the news! Our glorious forces continue to pound the insurgents on the Eastasia Front and victory is near. And, in a startling turnabout, actress Marilynn Sombee married Our Dear Leader's son, in a private ceremony in the East Wing of the Blue House. Former President O'Bummer was present, as was the State Clown, Chuckles. In weather news, we had a report that 1.33 inches of rain fell per minute in Uniontown, but since there is evidence that even more rain fell 233 million years ago at an even more impressive rate, this event seen in this context, is barely worth mentioning as it falls into the normal rainfall pattern over the last 4.32 bullion years of the planet. So the idea of global warming is still a hoax. And lastly, the sale of the century is happening at Mollifer's Food and Ammo store on Fifth and Laumbaugh. This is an amazing sale and constitutes one of the greatest events of merchandizing in the last 10,000 years. It is, of course, against the law not to attend one of these sales events, so get out, get in line early and have your national ID cards ready to show to indicate you are citizens worthy of these bargains. And that's all the news you can have for now. Please stand for the national anthem."

The image of the announcer faded out, replaced by the Emblem of the Republic, a twisted cross composed of 90 red triangles over a white and blue vertically-striped background.

Marcos and Maria stood, hands over their hearts, singing the anthem, never knowing when or if the camera embedded in the 3D holoscreen was watching.

After the mandatory participation was over, the screen switched to the state-sanctioned Hour of Your Favorite Commercials. For reasons even he could not fathom, Marcos went over to the bookshelf and brought back an ancient text, something he had had with him since he was a lad. He flipped the book open and whispered, "My name is Ozymandias, king of kings/Look on my works, ye Mighty, and despair!"

He then closed the book and immediately heard a strident screech from the television, "AZUL, MARCOS, SOOPER SHOPPER I.D. NUMBER 2011AA2 GENERATION CROCHITY, PUT THAT BOOK ON THE TABLE!"

Marcos did.

Within seconds, a searing blast of white shot out of the television. The book ignited, then exploded into smoke and vaporized verse.

It was as I suspected, Marcos thought. How long had they been under surveillance? He knew what was to happen next. He had heard about it. *They always let you think for a few minutes that you got away with it, that nothing would really happen.* Slowly, he turned, going into the bedroom, Maria following him. Then, quickly, he rolled the rug back, yanked up the trap door, then into the crawl space, scrambling into the tunnel and that tunnel joining another tunnel. In the distance they heard the screech of jets, the shuddering explosion of what once was their home and then, joining another family, they descended abruptly at a steep angle and kept moving some dozen yards more until they knew they were under—and well past—the border.

2

Not long after, Marcos and Maria sat on the porch of their new home on a bluff, south of the border of what Once Was That Great Country Up North. How they got to this place was a blur of memory, of detail, but shared love and heroism. After they arrived at this place, they often sat on the porch. They even had an extension built around to the north so they could admire, on the horizon and to the northeast, the ghostly aurora borealis-like glow of pinks, reds and yellows that hung over the hellish remnants of the vaporized Country Up North.

And Marcos and Maria grieved. They grieved, grieved, and *grieved*. The loss of their ancestors' dreams, the loss of their dreams, but, oh, oh, the loss of the dreams of That Country Up North that had been perceived by so many as "the ultimate, most hopeful place for humanity." The melting of the Statue of Freedom, the thermonuclear device detonated at Mount Rushless by Patriots for the Eradication of Liberals—everything their ancestors yearned for, that Marcos and Maria and the dreams of their ancestors actualized, lived, taken away from them and, now gone—gone, lost, forever.

They sat often, saying little, but as if sharing the same memories of sitting in the sewer pipe not far from the border, then, that night, helped by their aunts, their cousins, to steal away, though, they realized, they really had little to worry about since obviously that Once Great County Up North didn't particularly care about them in the first place, and would care less now, would be glad they were gone, and had no interest in pursuit—but the pain of being so cast out, uncared for, unwanted—seen as sub-human and when that Country Up North finally imploded by the nightmare replacing the dream—

Fidalgo, brother of Maria, often came to visit. After

brothers and cousins helped Marcos and Maria settle into their new home in the little town of Corazon, he often said, "Si, es verdad el filmo is ficion de ciencia pero *Forbidden Planet* —es una pilicula que neseceta a ver to understand el Pais del Norte. Los personas que vivian alli—son los Krell! Si no puede comprendar su ionconsciencias, si no aceptar su inconsciencia, que expectan usted? Que expectan? Caramba! Es obvio!"

Marcos might sigh. "Es hubrisimo. 'Mi nombre es Ozymandias'—" Then he might shake his head. "Denial. Denial of the unconscious. Denial of mortality. And like a monster from your wildest nightmare, reality bites, drags you down, goes for the throat."

Fidalgo would nod. "Si. Si. Que expectan? Que expectan?" And having a cerveza, they might sit on the north side of the porch, looking off to the horizon, to the shimmering curtains of color, of reds and orange over the graveyard of the Once Great Country Up North.

After the worst of the grieving was over, Marcos and Maria looked around to where they were now. Perhaps it was because the worst of the grieving was over. Or perhaps it just became numb after a while, and time was moving on.

One morning, sitting on the porch, sipping coffee, now looking east, sitting less frequently on the porch facing north, they looked over the dusty land to the shimmering distance under that soundless blue dome of heaven. Marcos was still surprised how good the coffee tasted now, and that the sweetener he used didn't create minute mushroom clouds in the coffee or make it taste so strange. Maria sat next to him, now smiling secretly again, wearing a beautiful white cotton dress, the sleeves embroidered with thread the color of the sea.

Marcos stood, drained his coffee, and picked up Maria's empty coffee cup off the wide, flat-topped railing in front of them on the open porch. "Mas?"

She nodded, smiled demurely. "Si, por favor?"

He went in, returned, set her coffee down, then, with saucer and cup, and slowly, as if measuring every movement, stepped down the three steps to the gravel driveway and surveyed the scene about him—to the Verana house across the dusty street where Mr. Verana, once a food chemist for Tao Chemical ("Until I discovered they were using my research to figure out how to create amnesia and alter attention spans and create fear in the population of That Country Up North—and it looks like they succeeded—" he once said) frequently brought over naturally modified fruit—from marble-sized watermelons to five kilo strawberries and an occasional pineapple that, when sliced open, was never the same color inside: red, blue, striped. Still tasted good. Marcos didn't ask questions. Verana gave no answers, just a grin, happy to share, then back to doing whatever he was doing to have more fun with fruit.

He looked down the street toward the dusty and beige-colored town of Corazon, past the home of the Phantasia family and little Chico who had some sort of strange biological condition which, while he was of normal health and healthy-looking, made him so light that, at times, when he was flying a kite, it took someone else to fly it with him lest he and the kite become airborne.

"Buenos dias Señor Azul—" came a far-away voice, and looking up, Marcos saw Chico dangling from a bright red kite—airborne as was the case today.

Marcos waved. "Tiene usted ciudado!"

"Si!" Chico yelled back, "Caramba! Yo veo Lago Corazon!"

Marcos watched Chico excitedly wave his arm and point but in his excitement, he lost grip of the kite string. Happily, the breeze abruptly died and like a feather, Chico gently floated down to earth.

Marcos laughed, sipped his coffee, then looked to the peaceful Corazon—a place of neighbors, families, a community, on the surface, a town that looked like beige blocks tossed on a dusty rug. A town that looked *pobre*, but beneath that impression, a wealth of love, of richness that was immeasurable, as broad as it was deep and to himself, he thought, *Yes, Yes. This is the day.* He sipped the coffee again, turned around, and walked up to the house and sat with Maria and realized that in the time he had been away, she had begun to knit a bright blue baby's jumper.

"You were out there," and she laughed, "and you decided it was time for a baby."

"I guess I did."

"Well. My body heard you and now I'm going to have a baby. It's a boy. While I was sitting here, he somehow told me that. Somehow he told his name was Pablo—but—"

"But?"

Maria patted her stomach. "I can't be sure, but somehow I think he wants to know if it's all right that he's sad."

Marcos laughed. "Tell him it's all right. Sad, happy, he'll be loved. You just tell him that."

Maria closed her eyes. Relaxed. After a minute she opened them. "I think he feels appreciation."

3

And so, nine months passed. Nine months with Pablo in Maria's belly, and she wept. "Oh, oh, oh," she kept saying through her tears, "He's so sad. So, so—trieste, azul. Oh, oh, so *so* sad."

Marcos did not know what to do. Dutifully he emptied out the buckets filled by Maria's tears during the night and she sat on the porch and wept during the day. Curiously, around the home, unbelievable as it was, blue grass grew and bright blue flowers bobbed in the wind. They rather looked like daisies, with pale blue petals and a deep blue center and blue leaves with a greenish hue, Marcos assumed, due to at least some chlorophyll that would have to be present.

The town doctor, Doctor Ojoslargos, was chagrined. "Merde," he often said, "never seen anything like it. Usually women have postpartum blues after the child is born. She's got prepartum blues or prepartum something."

Dr. Ojoslargos was a beef of a man with a round face and white hair that seemed to always be falling over his forehead. His gray eyes had the clarity of a microscope and seemed to regard everyone he met like they were a specimen of interest and he wondered where to catalog them. He loved red ties and was fond of letting you know that he studied in Paris, although he *never* said exactly where in Paris he studied. He always had this sense of unflappability, except when it came to Maria, where he was clearly and truly frustrated.

"Well," he said at one point, "if they still made antidepressants, she'd be a good candidate, but it's more like she needs a dam or to start a diet of sponges. Merde. I just don't know."

Maria shook her head. "I don't think these are even my tears," she wailed, "it's the sadness of Pablo."

"How can that possibly be?" said Dr. Ojoslargos, sitting in a chair next to hers on the porch. "He hasn't even been *born* yet. No fair crying until you at least open your eyes and see what kind of world this is—although," he straightened and looked about, "it's not *that* bad. At least not here. At least not now. I would think he should be happy, still rocking gently in your womb and enjoying the warmth of the amniotic fluid. He'll have enough to cry about when he is born. If anything, he should be crying tears of joy that he's not born yet." He puffed out his cheeks. "Be that as it may be about this vale of tears—well, just keep the buckets handy and when it gets time for your water to break—actually," he smiled, "can't imagine after nine months there would be any water left to break— but—well, maybe he'll be happy when he is born."

And he went on his way and that was pretty much how the conversations went those nine months.

And when the day did come that Pablo was born, he was rushed to the hospital, but as soon as Maria went through the doors of the hospital, they turned a pale blue. And going down the hallway to the delivery room, the walls changed from white to deeper and deeper shades of blue. And once in the delivery room, even the bright lights took on a curious shade of blue as did the skin of the nurses and their white smocks. Even the chrome instruments glittered and sparkled bright blue.

"Dios mio," said one nurse, "Un niño de milagro!"

Another nurse, an older, wiser woman, turned. "Si, si, pero que typo de milagro?"

"No estoy seguro."

But the birth went on. Pablo emerged with an immense gush as if he'd come out of a basin of water.

Dr. Ojoslargos gave Pablo a smart smack on the butt and Pablo let out a cry. Really. Truly. A cry. Not "Wahahhhhh," but a sobbing, "Wha-wha-*(hic)*-wha-wha—"

"Merde!" whispered Dr. Ojoslargos under his breath. "If we could just float him like a cloud, we'd never have to worry about our crops ever again. Ever."

And Pablo cried. And cried. And *cried.*

Once home, the crying seemed to die down when he slept, to a soft but never ending whimper and the tears were maybe a bit less. Maybe.

"Well," said Marcos to a fitfully sleeping Pablo at one point, "at least you're not crying—at least not as much."

Maria sat in the big soft bed off the kitchen on the main floor. "Yes, that is true," she said, and she looked down at Pablo nursing and whimpering, nursing and whimpering, "but I feel sad for him. Pobrecito. So much sadness to be born with. Where oh where did it all begin?"

Marcos sat on the bed, feeling it give. He ran his hand across the turquoise-colored bedspread, looked to Maria under the covers, Pablo *suckling whimpering suckling whimpering* at her right breast. "Maybe he knows something we can't know at our birth, maybe he has some foreknowledge that we don't want to—or can't acknowledge," he said slowly, and in a very measured, thoughtful way. "Maybe he's one of those who knows at the moment of conception that this is a one-way ticket to our demise. Maybe he's crying for the exquisite pain of being alive only to know one's death, that soon life will be gone."

Maria looked at Marcos. "Could he know that? How could he know that?"

Marcos shrugged. "What do we really know?" asked Marcos. "What if the Buddhists are right? That reincarnation exists? But what if there's a mistake and a spirit comes into this life knowing of his past life? Maybe Pablo is remembering how he died? And he's still grieving it?"

"Dios mio," whispered Maria.

"What if Pablo is a spirit that has skipped generations and he was a cave man being trampled by a woolly mammoth? And he's remembering that!"

Maria looked truly alarmed. "Oh, my—" she looked down at Pablo. *Suckle whimper suckle whimper.*

"—or what if—" and Maria's dark eyes grew wide in wonderment and horror, "what if his spirit is from another— another planet—and he saw his family destroyed in a space attack and he saw his parents die, then he was killed—"

Marcos shook his head at the possibilities. "Or he came here from a different dimension and with his birth, he's going to try to seek a way back to his other world?"

Maria looked down again at Pablo. "The possibilities," she whispered, "the possibilities of the origin of his pain and tears is as big as—as—the universe!"

Marcos looked up, his gaze shifting in the direction of the Once Great Country Up North. "What if his tears are about the generations of peoples striving for an idea of freedom—only to see it snatched away—that would certainly be something worth crying about—worth crying about forever."

Maria, softly, "What if this is about the pain of our ancestors who struggled, fought for a better life, sacrificed so much, had it—then lost it—" She looked up beseechingly to Marcos. "Even I feel sad, terribly, *terribly* sad about that."

Marcos ran his fingers through his hair then sighed, slapped his hands to his thighs in frustration. "And the damnable thing is that it's all conjecture, all speculation, all fantasy—we can't possibly know until he can talk."

Maria brushed her fingers across Pablo's brow as he *suckled whimpered suckled whimpered*. "I know," she whispered, "I know. Until then, maybe as he grows, he can point to things."

"But didn't he tell you what he needed at the moment of conception? Didn't he ask if it was all right if he cried?"

"Well," and Maria looked hesitant and a bit confused, "I thought he did." She bit her lip. "Well, he didn't actually say—it was more of a sense—but it was only then—it was like he wanted permission to be sad without knowing why, and then that took over and drowned out everything else."

Marcos sighed, ran his fingers through his hair once more. Then, with resignation, put both hands on his thighs again and said, "It is what it is. If we but knew, we could help him. Then he brightened a bit. "Can you relax enough to try to contact him again?"

Maria thought for a moment. "Because he was a part of me I could much more easily experience him, even though it was overwhelming sadness. But now he's apart from me— but—" She thought a moment more, then closed her eyes in concentration. After a few minutes, she opened them again. "Just sadness. Less because he's outside my body, but—still sadness."

Marcos stood, came over to Maria and ran his hand down her hair, then over Pablo's head. "Such sadness," he said. "Such profound sadness. Someday we will understand."

He gathered up a plate, a cup emptied of tea, and took them to the kitchen and stopped at the doorway.

Suckle whimper suckle whimper.

Someday, he thought, *someday we will understand. Sooner rather than later, I hope. Ai!*"

4

Those days that were to lead to *someday* seemed unending. But in spite of the constant crying of Pablo Azul, such tears did have certain benefits. Happily, their water bill was drastically reduced since Pablo's tears filled so many buckets, the water was recycled to flush the toilet, water the plants in the garden, wash the dishes and made for fine soups that didn't require too much salt. And perhaps it was just coincidence that there was more humidity in the air over Corazon and lo and behold, at times clouds, though definitely with a blue cast, covered the skies, and there was a ten percent increase in precipitation. And the sky was definitely, most definitely, bluer.

Through the first two years, Marcos was fond of saying, "Not so bad. We still don't know why he's sad, but—" he shrugged, pointing to the lawn that was certainly well-watered, but nonetheless had a definite blue glow to it, "—not so bad."

One morning, while drinking coffee with Marcos, Maria said, "Even if he's sad, there is still beauty in it and he is certainly a beautiful boy. I just hope he doesn't spend all his life crying. Certainly there must be some joy coming his way."

On this particular morning, while Marcos and Maria sipped coffee and shared their observations, Pablo was sitting in the middle of the lawn, crying, crying, crying. A white moth fluttered by and, upon passing Pablo, turned bright blue. And after a while, the grass grew up around him, then when it got too high, it gently fell against him, as if soothing him in a grassy caress.

"My," said Maria, "it's as if the world wants to comfort him."

Marcos sipped his coffee, then after a minute said, "Or else he and the world are in sympathy with each other."

Weeping, Pablo leaned forward and patted the lawn; white roses burst from the ground and then, becoming blue, gently,

gently rested their blossoms on his outstretched legs.

Pablo saw this and cried even more. Then over his head a little blue cloud formed and a faint, blue mist fell on Pablo's head gently, again, as if caressing him.

Maria turned to Marcos. "You know that Dr. Ojoslargos is coming by to check on Pablo. Tomorrow. I really don't have anything new to report about his behavior, do you?"

Marcos sighed. "No. Nothing unusual." For a few minutes, he simply looked to Pablo, then pushed his hat back and squinted into the distance, into the bright hot and white of the day, and said, "Sure wish the pobrecito would talk."

After a minute, Maria said, "Are you still going into town to look for work?"

"Guess I should. Guess eventually the good money we made in that Country Up North had to run out, though it sure lasted down here." He smiled. "Amazing that when you have love and good friends, you don't really need much beyond that. When the Friendly Peoples F-18 MIG Predators took out our house, you know all we escaped with was our money—we must have lost thousands of dollars worth of stuff—but—" he smiled, hugged Maria. "Don't miss it. Don't miss nada. Haven't bought much. Don't need much. Funny. What money we had from the job which I went to for twelve hours a day—would have lasted us maybe a month up there—down here, it's kept us going for two years. Amazing how little you need." He shook his head. "Been much happier down here. Replacing love with *stuff* isn't a life. But what I don't understand is —if we're happier, why is Pablo so— blue?"

Maria just nodded. "Dr. Ojoslargos will be here tomorrow. Maybe he'll know."

"Maybe so, maybe so." He stood. "Well, off to see if I can find work. If I got a job one day a week, I think that would do it."

Maria just smiled.

When Marcos returned home several hours later, he was smiling.

Maria, in the kitchen, fixing a lunch for a wailing Pablo, glanced over to Marcos. "Hello, I bet you got a job."

"Sure did." said Marcos, sitting at the kitchen table across from Pablo, who looked at his father and burst out afresh in tears. "Yes, got a job at the employment center helping people find jobs."

"Dios Mio," said Maria. She poured Marcos a glass of milk and brought it to him. Pablo looked at the milk. It turned a lovely shade of—blue. Pablo wept, great tears rolling down his face.

Marco took a sip. "Went into the office and got to talking to the gentleman behind the desk and he finally said that I sure had a way about me and asked me to fill in for him."

"Que bueno," said Maria. "Dr. Ojoslargos can't come tomorrow but said he could come today. Is that all right?"

"Sure, sure, si, si."

There was a knock on the door. "Buenos tardes," came the voice of Dr. Ojoslargos.

"Enter," said Marcos, "Quire usted leche? Una beer? Whiskey?"

"Merde," said Doctor Ojoslargos, "you sure know how to tempt un hombre. But can't drink on company time." He looked at his watch. "Off company time. Beer?" He pulled out a chair from the table. The cat, Blue Dwarf, hissed, sprang from the chair and slipped into a bright opening in the space-time continuum where he wouldn't be bothered for whatever time frame he needed to create.

"Una cerveza para usted," said Marcos. He went over to the refrigerator, which was a fine and elegant shade of blue, and brought out two beers. He opened them and poured out the contents of one bottle for Dr. Ojoslargos. The beer formed a sphere.

Marcos looked down to where Blue Dwarf had vanished and saw a vertical sliver of white in the air. "Blue Dwarf!" said Marcos. "Shut the portal!"

A faint and distant 'yowl' and the sliver of light vanished. Maria shook her head. "Blue Dwarf always does that." She brought over two glasses, deftly slipping one under the sphere of beer floating some inches above the table in front of the doctor. After a minute, the local space-time normalized, the beer lost its spherical gravity cohesion, and plopped into the glass.

"Gatos," said Marcos, then poured beer into his glass.

"Well," said the doctor looking at Pablo. "No changes I assume?"

Marcos sipped his beer. "Nope. Nada different. El Mismo. Crying. Lots of tears. Caramba. Muchos tears."

The doctor nodded. He tapped a finger against the glass of beer, then took a sip himself. "Been thinking," he finally said. "How much in the way of volume does he produce?"

Marcos scratched his head and looked to Maria, who looked something of a loss. "Muchos buckets. I don't know how he does it. It's like he has the hose from the ocean in him, the way those tears come out."

"Lots of tears left over from your daily use?"

Marcos nodded. Sipped his beer. Nodded again. "Si. Muchos."

"Well," said Doctor Ojoslargos, adjusting his tie which referenced a long-gone city in that corpse of that Once Great Country Up North, which read, "SeaYaTul Rain Festival, November 30th to October 31st." "Just want you to think about it. Those leftover tears might make a good soup stock. Who knows? Might make a lot of money."

Marcos nodded. "We'll definitely think about it. Thank you for thinking of us."

The doctor took a drink of beer and sighed. "Hate to waste a good thing, sabe?"

Marcos sipped his beer. Then, "Si. Es la verdad." Then, "Have to think about it. Tal vez un corporation? *Terars de Pablo Para Sopa?*"

Dr. Ojoslargos simply smiled. "Hablaramos mas de eso but it is un bueno idea." He drained his beer. "Gracias."

"Quire usted un otro?"

But Dr. Ojoslargos shook his head. "No, gracias. Back on company time."

He got up. Glanced to a whimpering Pablo who, upon seeing the doctor look at him, broke out afresh in deep sobs.

"Merde" said the doctor, "que estrange. Such a mystery. Time will tell. Keep me, of course, apprised if anything out of the ordinary happens." He stopped, snapped his fingers. "Almost forgot. Been meaning to do this." He reached inside his thin, pale blue coat and pulled out five plastic specimen bottles from an inside pocket. "Want to get samples of Pablo's tears. Maybe we can find something in them that is causing this malady. If nothing else, maybe these tears contain something that could increase fuel efficiency for automobiles. Maybe a cure for a disease. I will send samples out to the Instituto de Ciencies and have them research it. And may well send samples to the Aeronautcio Nacional y Administration Para Exploracion de Espaca. You never know. Quein sabe?"

He went over to Pablo, who was still whimpering, crying. Seeing the doctor, he broke out in fresh tears. Seconds later, the doctor had the specimen bottles filled to the brim. He capped them, put them back in his coat pocket. "Quien sabe?" he said. "Quien Sabe? You never, never know. The power of a child's tears."

"Thank you," said Marcos, shaking the doctor's hands. "Thank you for being so interested and so helpful with Pablo."

"Gracias," said Maria, smiling, every hopeful look in her eyes mixed with gratitude that, to Marcos, seemed to say that at least they weren't the only ones who didn't understand what was going on.

"De nada. Until later." He waved and went on his way, the *thump-thump-thump* of his heavy footfall fading away on the porch while Pablo sat and cried; his tears finally forming a little torrent that flowed across the table and cascaded off the edge, not far from where Blue Dwarf had vanished. Suddenly, Marcos and Maria observed a bright blue flash, mid-air, then Blue Dwarf leaped out, ears back, hissing. Little planets orbited his head, a silver one and a ringed one and a blue water world with gleaming polar caps. With typical feline irritation, Blue Dwarf swatted at them and they went flying off.

"Poor kitty," said Maria. "Pablo's tears must have shorted out the circuits in the dimensional fields."

Marcos just shrugged. "Quien sabe?" He watched Blue Dwarf take off, chasing a comet. "Gatos!" He laughed.

And Pablo cried.

5

And Pablo continued to cry, and the older he got, the more he cried. By age five, he had actually become quite the story in Corazon and in the Southern Lands. Even El Presidente de la Republic, Presidente Kennedente, sent him a note wishing him well and that he would follow his progress and hoped for the best. In the local media, the story was carried, the speculations abounded, and the strange occurrences in the land were increasingly attributed to Pablo and his tears. The bright blue sparking mists in the town of Alma, some thirty kilometers distance, while strange, graciously left the town cool even on the hottest of days, and brought more than a little appreciation from the townspeople, who were only too happy for the cool weather, but also more than happy to attribute it to Pablo. In the town of Amor, some ten kilometers to the north, the recent invasion of dark caterpillars that then went into the pupa stage only to release moths with minute blue diamonds in their wings were an amazing show of beauty and strangeness. When the villagers captured them and took them to the capitol of the region—*milagros!* Foreign investors paid fantastic prices and villagers who went to the capitol poor came back driving top of the line Jaguars. And the water tables, always something of an uncertainty in the area, were now high and supplying a flow of dependable, bright blue water.

Indeed, the region had become such a place of wealth that anonymous donations came to the Azul household as well as outright grants, and gifts and public acclaim from the "El Niño Azul de Milagros."

And no matter how much adulation, no matter how much attention, enough to make anyone else dizzy with delight and possibilities, Pablo Azul just kept crying.

And in all of this, Marcos, Maria, Dr. Ojoslargos, as well as visiting psychiatrists from Lima and Buenos Aires—even a famous hypnotist-writer with his cartooning girlfriend, having escaped from a seaport city in the northwest, the city of S. by the mountains, by the sea, a city that, along with that Country Up North, no longer existed, even with his credentials, could not understand the endless flow of tears from Pablo Azul and of course, Little Pablo, at his age, could hardly be expected to have the insight to understand why he was so sad.

But Marcos and Maria, they never stopped loving him, and trying to understand his deep and unending source of immense lament.

Very often Maria would just sit with Pablo and simply say, "Que? Porque es triest?"

And Pablo, unable to put it into words, wept anew.

Maria would ruffle his hair. "Mi niño, se puede—" She took his right arm, then his first finger, and began pointing at things. "The sky?" she asked.

Pablo nodded. And wept.

"Flowers?"

Pablo nodded. And wept.

Blue Dwarf came prancing through the blue-hued grass, leaping and swatting at a red and white striped bumblebee with blue wings. "Blue Dwarf?"

"Wha-wha-wha-whaaaa—" sobbed Pablo.

Maria spread her hands. "*Everything?* Todos el mundo?"

And Pablo wept anew. Although Maria thought this might be an answer, the crying was neither more nor less than it ever was. But what was obvious to her, to Marcos, the doctor, and everyone else was this: the older Pablo became, the more he grew—and *so* did the quantity of tears.

Before Pablo was six, Marcos had to dig a trench to drain away the excess tears that poured from Pablo's eyes. Before long, this drainage, of course, turned into a fairly sizable creek that coursed through the front yard of the Azul home, ran down alongside the main road, flowed into a culvert that went under the new cement highway, only to join a literal fountain of water furiously bubbling and roiling up from a water table so near the surface—indeed, so near the surface, that springs soon began bubbling up everywhere, flowing to what had been a historically dry river bed near the city, full only during rare flash floods—now it ran full, all the time, year round, running so full that it began to nibble at the edges of roadways and spilling into yards. And there was the matter of the town directly downstream, the town of Dormir.

One day not long after Pablo turned seven and a particularly large part of the road between Dormir and Corazon had washed way, the Mayor of Dormir, Mr. Sueño, paid the Azul family a visit.

Marcos and Maria greeted him while Pablo sat on the front steps weeping, weeping, weeping, his little balled fists raised to his eyes, torrents running down, soaking the blue swimming trunks that Maria kept him dressed in these days.

"I am the mayor of—"

"Dormir," said Marcos. "Dormir y Sonar, ai, that's the rub," said Marcos, sounding somewhat philosophical.

Mr. Sueño was a tall, broad-shouldered man with a beak of a nose. He was dressed in a white shirt that abruptly turned pale blue when Pablo glanced his way. Somewhat unnerved, Mr. Sueño nonetheless squared his shoulders, took off his straw hat, revealing thinning black hair turning to gray. "Yes, well, I've heard Shakespearean references before," said Mr. Sueño, "unfortunately, all too often. But be that as it may be, and given how appreciative we are for the many gifts your son's tears have brought us for which we are truly grateful—and—" he cleared his throat, clearly uncomfortable, "I do not wish to be or appear ungrateful, for we have certainly benefited in Dormir—our reservoirs are full, our new lakes brimming with fish, and the huge valley not far away which has not seen a lake in three million years is now full. For this we are grateful. Our lawns are green and every morning we are blessed with a fine blue mist rolling in off the little ocean and our climate is so agreeable but, well—" he twisted the brim of his hat in his hands, "the river is getting pretty full and we wonder if you've found any basis for the tears so that maybe he could cry just a bit less? At least until the water table goes down a bit? Some? Just a little? Un poquito?" He held up one hand, with the thumb and forefinger barely apart.

Marcos held his hands up in a helpless gesture. "Surely you've read the papers and tuned into the local media—it's a mystery. If we could turn off his waterworks, we would, but only Pablo knows—but at age seven he can't possibly know. His personal insight into his sadness may be years, decades away."

Mr. Dormir swallowed, obviously ill at ease. "But—but—but—at the rate he's growing and crying, he could wash us all away. What if he *really* gets sad and releases a flash flood of tears and it overwhelms the channel and takes out the new dam we've had to construct—"

Marcos again shrugged his shoulders in a "what can you

do" show of resignation.

"Can you take him to the Sahara Desert? Certainly there's enough sand to soak up his tears for. . ."

He trailed off as Maria handed a newspaper to Marcos, who then pointed out a headline to Mr. Dormir: "Vast Lake Forms in What Was the Sahara Desert."

"Well, there's the Atacama Desert, driest place in—"

Maria gave another paper to Marcos, who opened it to page A3 and the headline that read, "Vast Inland Sea Forms in Atacama Desert from Unprecedented Rains from Odd Blue Clouds—Scientists Stumped."

Mr. Dormir tried again. "Move to the coast?"

Another paper. "Unexplained Rapid Sea Level Rise, Major Port Cities Underwater."

"Somewhere?"

Marcos looked to Maria and she looked back to him. They both shrugged in helplessness. "Donde?"

The Mayor sat hard in a chair at the table. For a few minutes, his mouth worked like he was a fish out of water. "But—but—if all this is true—caramba, the oceans will continue to rise and we—we—we're all going to drown in su hjios tears. We—you we have to do *something*."

"Well," said Marcos, with great resignation, "we're hoping for a moment of insight when he can finally tell us what this is all about, that the tears will stop when he puts his sadness into words."

Mayor Dormir shook his head in disbelief. "—but you said yourself that could take—take—forever—years—what if he doesn't get insight soon enough? And who has insight until they're older? Thirty? Forty? At the rate the oceans are rising, we'll drown in months! Already, the brewery in town has been flooded and we've been out of Blackhole Stout and Porter Cervaza for a week—do you have any idea how difficult it is to rule a town with sober citizens who can't get their cerveza? Have pity on us!"

At this display of emotion, Pablo, who was outside, began to *really,* cry and there was the distant but thunderous roar of a mighty waterfall.

"Please," said, Marcos, "please, give us time. We are doing all we can do."

"I certainly hope so." And with that, Mayor of Dormir, Mr. Sueño, got up and left.

"*Ai,*" sighed Marcos. "That's the rub."

6

Dr. Ojoslargos visited several days later; he came up the steps, pausing briefly to ruffle the hair of sobbing Pablo. He came in through the open door. "Buenos dias," he said. Today he was dressed in a pale blue suit and wore a dark shirt with bright red tie.

Marcos, seated at the kitchen table with Maria, stood, came over and shook his hand.

"Off company time," the doctor announced, grinning.

Marcos went over to the fridge and got out several beers and poured them into pale blue glasses. Maria sat, sipping coffee.

"I wanted to see you today," said the doctor, "because I've been looking over all these notes we've taken about your lad. I've talked to many specialists and I think we have a diagnosis. "Prenatal Melancholia with Postpartum Globalization of Melancholia—which means—" he stopped with a look of, 'well, here goes,' "looks like he was born sad, and once born, looked around to the world, saw what a mess it was, so it just reinforces his sadness."

Marcos looked to Maria, Maria to Marcos. "Bien. But why was he born sad?"

"Just don't know that. But the point of this is—" And Dr. Ojoslargos sighed, "each state reinforces the other; in other words, his crying is simply beyond his control. En otros palabras, it's doubtful it's going to stop."

Marcos tapped the tabletop with his fingers. "Well, certainly there was a lot to be sad about before his birth; all the pain of our ancestors, the destruction of hope, the decay of the planet, *ai*, what is there not to be sad about?"

"Be that as it may be," said the doctor, then taking a drink, "no matter how much insight he gets, it may never stop the waterworks. He'll always find something to be sad about, to cry about. No matter what. It's his nature to be sad. Born sad, living sad. And meanwhile—" He took from his briefcase the daily paper. The headlines read: "Ocean Level Rise Critical. Australia Flooding." "Something Has to Be Done."

Marcos rubbed his brow, closed his eyes. Maria came over to him, placed her hands on his shoulders.

"As if we don't know that," sighed Marcos. "As if we haven't known that for what, seven years?" He continued to lean forward, rubbing his forehead. "Nesescitos una milagro. Oh, que we need es una milagro. Pronto. Soon. Now!"

"Indeed," said Dr. Ojoslargos. "Indeed. Maybe we can talk to someone we haven't talked to before. Maybe—maybe— something technological—something—"

He drained his glass. Laughed. "Back on company time!" He stood and left.

That evening, with the sounds of rushing water and immense geysers in the distance and Pablo sobbing, sobbing, sobbing, and Blue Dwarf flying off the porch to snatch unsuspecting blue flashing fireflies from the air, Marcos sat on the porch. Then, getting up, he went into the yard, looked up to the sky with the swath of the Milky Way like a river of sparkling frost and he took off his hat, held it in reverence and, looking up at the sky in a manner beseeching, humble and hopeful, he said, "Dios Mio, I've not been a very religious man, maybe in my heart but I've never spoken to you in all my forty-two years. But I know you sent us Pablo, our tearful and sad Pablo here for a purpose. If we just knew what it was. We know he was born sad and with good reason. So much to be sad about. And I look around to what we have done to your crown jewel of a world and I am so ashamed. I can understand the tears of Pablo. It is so sad. And now I see we face drowning not just from glaciers melting but also from Pablo's tears. I cannot believe this is the fate of him, of us. He doesn't deserve to drown in his own grief and so many don't." Marcos felt the sting of tears. He looked up to the stars, to the Milky Way, "If I just knew—if I could just know what—" He stopped. He just—stopped. Then fell to his knees, hands tightly clasped together and gasped, "Un milagro," he said to the Universe, "You have given me a miracle and had I just looked up before—yes, yes, Dios Mio, yes, it is true—ask and you shall receive."

He abruptly felt the presence of Maria beside her hand on his shoulders. "Dear husband, esta bein? Que pasa?"

Still staring at the the night sky, Marcos said, "Yes, yes, I've never been so well in my life."

"—que?"

But Marcos just said, "Mas tarde, must make a phone call, must call the doctor! Ahora!" He dashed inside and called Dr. Ojoslargos who simply said, in an astonished and hushed voice, "Merde! Que una idea brilliante! Brilliante. Yes, yes, Manana."

The next day, the doctor came over and met Marcos and Maria on the porch. Pablo wept nearby and what was once a spare creek, now a gushing river on the other side of the road, was now threatening to take out the road.

The Doctor said, "Yes, quite the idea and I made phone calls and with the monies and grants we have, we can do this. We can do this. We leave tomorrow morning. Pack lightly; everything will be provided. This just might work."

"No other choices," said Marcos. He shook his head. "It's

either this or drown."

Maria just stood nearby, somber and nodding slowly,

Dr. Ojoslargos gave a short laugh. "That's exactly right." He looked over to Pablo, dressed in a sopping blue t-shirt and shorts and crying, "No choice. *Ai!* None. Merde!" He abruptly turned and went to his car, a blue, classic Barracuda.

At nine the next morning, Dr.Ojoslargos came over in an open jeep. The Azuls loaded it with a few incidentals, a suitcase filled with clothes, several books, and empty pails for the tears of Pablo who, crying, climbed in the back of the jeep with Maria.

Dodging washouts and several minor flashfloods, they made it to the airport at the capitol and waited. Pablo sat in the jeep and sobbed.

"Hard to leave again?" asked the doctor.

"Always hard to leave," said Marcos. He put his hands in the pockets of his jeans, and noticed that his white shirt with pearl buttons was slowly changing to a turquoise blue. Maria emptied several pails of tears on the tarmac.

Marcos was about to say something else when the doctor pointed to the south. Like a silver bird, like something sleek and elegant and wonderful, a ship, with elegant curved wings and slender body descended and, again, like a bird, seemed to gently fall from the sky, then with wheels extending, landed, rolled a short distance, and stopped not far away. The doctor and Pablo and Marcos and Maria hurried over to the ship. In a minute, the door slid open and a ladder descended. A gentleman, dressed in a pilot's uniform, which looked rather military: beige (slowly taking on a bluish hue) and festooned with many medals, climbed down the ladder and once on the tarmac, turned and faced the four of them. The pilot was a tall and elegant-looking man, tanned but smooth-faced with mist-gray eyes that had an amazing clarity and depth. "Pilot Juan Luna." He shook their hands. "I am ordered by the Presidente de la Republic Presidente Kennedente, to thank you for this splendid idea. No cost. If this idea goes as we think, it will truly be a wonderful thing we can all be proud of. In his words, 'We are going on this mission, not because it is easy, but because it is hard.' We had to work quickly to make the changes specified for—" and he looked at a sobbing Pablo, still sitting in the jeep, "our tearful passenger, but we did it. It has become well known to our scientists that the tears of this child mixed with rocket fuel tremendously enhance the efficiency of said fuel and we estimate that this may accelerate rockets by 91.4 percent on deep space missions. With Pablo on board we can discover just how much of his tears we need to make this so. And also, we need to discover if fresh tears will make a difference in the duration on the journey. So please, up the ladder and welcome aboard."

In minutes, the Azuls and Doctor Ojoslargos were seated; Pablo at the window next to Maria, then a blue, carpeted aisle way, and two more seats with Marcos and the Doctor at the window. There were six rows behind them; several technicians in deep, blue uniforms sat at a console in back. Round, small windows were across from each other on either side of the cabin. The pilot closed the door to the cabin and stood at the front; behind him, a door to the cockpit. "Before you settle in," he said, "your belongings should go in the overhead compartments. Please buckle your shoulder harness and seat belts. This is the Republic Space Plane, the plans of which were delivered to us by engineers who, working for the DeltaBoing Aerospace Industries in that Once Great Country Up North, escaped before the attempted mass internment of its citizens when they refused to spend a weekend buying and consuming, which caused civil war and the empire to collapse. We, along with other countries down here, constructed five of these planes and so far, all have made it to the moon and back." He smiled to Pablo weeping uncontrollably. "We have for Pablo a special helmet with eye cups to catch the tears which will be funneled out into a special tubing which will lead to a reservoir which will feed directly into the rocket engine and we should be on our way as soon as young Pablo here cries enough tears. So," he looked to Pablo, "I'm going to help you with the eye cups—" He reached around behind him, producing a helmet and eye cups with tubes that came out from the bottom then joined as one tube that ended in a narrowed tip. He went over to Pablo, put the goggles on, then fit the end of the tube into a fixture in the wall of the cabin. "Now," he said, "the helmet will help block out sounds and light so you many continue your sadness and crying uninterrupted."

Maria, sitting next to him, said, "But he cries so much. Won't he drown in the helmet?" Protectively, she put her arm around Pablo's shoulders.

"Oh, no, no," said the pilot. "We have a negative airflow in the tubing which will help pull the tears along without backing up."

Pablo looked something like a frog with the goggles on and he wept out of confusion and uncertainty. "It's okay," said the pilot to Pablo. "This helmet will be helpful to you to keep you in your present feelings." He put the helmet on, plugged the end of the tube from the goggles into the wall outlet; uninterrupted, Pablo's shoulders moved about in abrupt little jerks, clearly indicating uncontrolled sobbing.

Maria buckled up Pablo then put her harness on as did Marcos and Dr. Ojoslargos. Another pilot, a short man with an efficient and calm demeanor, looked into the cabin, then disappeared with the pilot to the front of the ship.

In less than a minute, the pilot spoke over the intercom. "We now have the five liters of the child's tears we need to mix with the rocket fuel. We will be lifting off immediately. This technology is so advanced that it will only feel like a plane lifting off and then the slightest pressure as we gently cruise to the edge of space. Then you will feel an abrupt jolt as the main engines engage to take us into space. We will pass the moon in a few minutes. Then, if our theory is correct, we simply should just keep on accelerating. We've not gone to this speed before.

This will be a grand mission!"

And indeed, the flight was smooth, effortless, and to all the passengers, it was simply like riding an elevator.

"Unbelievable," said Marcos, "I'd always heard that such flight was horrible, and so painful. This is nothing."

Dr. Ojoslargos nodded. "I too am surprised. It's nothing. It's either very advanced technology or maybe—" he shrugged, "maybe it's the effect of a child's tears."

Before they knew it, the moon came into view and was gone, just flashing by. "Amazing," said Marcos. "Just like that... at the rate we are going and if we keep accelerating—"

The intercom clicked on. "As you know, we just passed the moon. We are not yet up to speed; that will happen in another hour. And in about seven hours, we will be at our destination. So, allow yourselves to be comfortable. Bathrooms are at the rear of the cabin; please grab the holds at the top of the seats as the gravity will be minimal. Snacks are in the plastisteel compartments; if you wish to drink something, please read the instructions on the containers. And the space sickness bags are in a compartment right under your seat and should you use one, *please* seal it tightly after use! Thank you!" There was a *click* as the intercom went off.

7

Pablo, of course, cried all through the journey, Though you couldn't see the tears or hear him cry, the way he moved, the jerking of the shoulders, nothing had changed. He was crying; the wracking sobs the same now as they had been all his life.

Marcos looked out the window and sure enough, their destination drew rapidly close. "That a child's tears could make a rocket be so powerful; to fly so far so fast," he said.

Dr. Ojoslargos nodded. "A child's tears are very powerful. But," he said, "we can't have him know or be surprised yet about where we are. We must keep him crying." He glanced out to the barren and dark lands of their destination that had been dead for so many millions of years, a land that once had life but had dried out, like a flower gone to seed and nothing remaining. He looked out. Such a desolate wasteland. So cold, so bleak, so far, so far, far away from Earth.

At that point, Pilot Luna came in and said to both Marcos and the doctor, "We are coming in close. In a few minutes, we will hit the upper atmosphere; right now, we have diverted the flow of Pablo's tears from the engines to the vents that will exhaust his tears to the outside where they will freeze and create ice crystals. Now you must make sure he cries—cries like he has *never*, ever cried before."

The doctor sighed and nodded, "Yes, yes. Now he really must cry and our destination, as exotic and strange as it may be, must not interfere with that." He massaged his forehead then looked up, thoughtful. "If this succeeds—" he stopped, looked away, and said in a philosophical tone, "What if all the sad children in the world have a chemistry in their tears similar to Pablo's—what a gift such children could give to the universe. And what immense joy would come from their grief."

Pilot Luna smiled. "Es posible. But first, we start with Pablo," he said, "We have positioned the ship so that he can't see anything. Yet. When the time is right, if we think what is going to happen *does* happen, we will bank the ship. Then Pablo will see what beauty has come from his sadness."

Marcos and Doctor Ojoslargos looked to each other. "Agreed," they said. Then Marcos glanced to Maria, who sat looking somber yet hopeful with a slight smile on her lips, nodding in agreement.

"We now have gravity," said Pilot Luna. "You may now move about the cabin."

Everyone unbuckled themselves from their harnesses; Marcos and Doctor Ojoslargos came over to sit behind Pablo and Maria. Maria gently released and removed Pablo's helmet. Pablo sat, eye protectors still in place, draining away the ever-flowing tears.

Marcos whispered to Pablo, "Ah, my son, my son, you were born crying, born weeping the tears of our ancestors who struggled, who dreamed, who sought a better life, only to find that the country they sought so hard to be a part of turned on them, cast them out like Adam and Eve from Eden. Cry, cry, my beloved son, cry. Cry for the planet dying at the hands of greed, and the animals and species dying, dying, an atmosphere choking and lands dying. Cry, cry my, beloved son, for a dying planet at the hands of greed." And Pablo did cry. Cried like he never cried before. "Cry, cry Pablo, for all the animals who had no say in their extinction. Cry for the los Indios whose only sin was being Indian, for the Incas whose only sin was being Incas; cry for the pain, for the loss, for a belief that life could truly be different but in the end, was not allowed to be different."

And Pablo cried. Cried for his ancestors, cried for the planet. Cried, cried and cried with great, deep wracking sobs. From where he was sitting, Marcos could see the tears of Pablo becoming pale blue mists and clouds outside, below the ship.

"And now, my son, I must tell you that we are now at our destination, a planet that once had water but now has none, that once had oceans but now only deserts, a planet with once blue sky but now only an atmosphere threadbare and sparse. Cry, cry my son, for what once was but is here no more. Cry, cry my son, for the dying of a planet so early in its life, for a promise that could not be kept. Cry, cry for the pain of life begun then the promise snatched away."

Marcos could feel the ship bank, turn, and below, he could see thick clouds forming from the tears of Pablo. And Pablo cried and wept, his tears being exhausted outside the ship at a rate that was unbelievable.

Marcos felt the ship turning again, now he looked over a sea of clouds, blue-black in the sky but on the eastern horizon, he saw dawn coming. Then they glided into the clouds—

"Look, Pablo." said Marcos. "Look. Look and prepare

to see what your tears have done. And be proud my son, be proud!"

Maria gently removed the goggles and lifted Pablo's chin; snuffling, Pablo looked out the window.

The ship glided down through the clouds, now lighter in the pre-dawn light, and then they dropped below the clouds—

All stared in stunned silence; Pablo gasped, for abruptly below and before them, a vast and rolling expanse of land, dark blue and green. Then the sun burst over the edge of the world; in the distance a vast and sudden sea flashed blue and bright, in the early morning Martian light.

Justice in Amerry-Ka

You see the giant spiders sitting at the bench. One is black. The other white. They play a game of chess. You've got really fine vision and you see that all the pieces on the board are—*you*. The spiders are dressed in judicial robes; the black one wears a white robe, the white one wears a black one. You have this intense sense of foreboding. Somehow this does not look good. Your lawyer stands beside you. He has eyes all over his body. You wonder how a lawyer could have so many eyes. "Comes with the profession," he once hissed. Your lawyer doesn't miss a thing. Not a fucking thing.

"Check," says the black spider in the white robes. "Your king is in check."

"I noticed," says the other spider.

"No matter what you do—"

"I know," says the spider dressed in black. "No matter what I do—"

"You move into check."

The white spider then turns to you. "Now, how do you plead?"

You don't know what to say.

"Say something," your lawyer says.

"What?"

"*Something!*"

"Something," you say.

"Guilty as charged," replies the spider in white.

Your lawyer rises in your defense. "But," he turns to you, "before I defend you any further, your case has already cost $78,000."

Internally, you crash. "But—but—but—" you whimper,

"I thought we'd discuss cost after the case—you said so— $78,000 is a lot to defend me—"

"You got it wrong—I changed my mind. I decided not to wait. And—" he smiles, "it's $78,000—*so far*."

"But—but—but you've only defended me for five minutes."

"Picky, picky, picky. Legal stuff is costly. Can you afford me or not?"

You don't know what to say. Mentally, you tally your assets: clothing: $50, wages: $100 dollars a day. House: 70% depreciation from the last, Corporate Managed Economic Adjustment— from $50,000 yesterday to now being worth only $5,000 today. You realize that, as far as affording this, you're fucked.

"There's no way I can afford this," you whisper.

"Tsk," says the lawyer. He ups and leaves. But of course, he leaves his bill: $79,000—while you were fretting, the cost went up $1,000.

The giant white spider in black robes leaps upon a large, unsuspecting fly and as it wraps the fly in silk, it says to you, "Does the witness wish to respond to the accusations before him?"

Somewhere, you regain enough strength to say, "I—I'd like to know the charges against me—"

"You should know them," says the spider in black, somehow focusing all his eight eyes on you.

"Maybe I should. But I don't."

The black spider in white robes sighs, or maybe it hisses. It's hard to say which. "Which of the many charges do you wish to hear?" It goes back to sucking the juices from the fly.

"All of them."

"Take too long," says the black-robed spider judge. "How about the best ones? I've got some outstanding ones that I've highlighted in yellow day-glow marker."

"That'd be fine."

"You were born."

You gulp. "But I can't help that."

"Guilty of Original Sin. Born Bad. Guilty as charged."

"M—may I hear the other charges?"

"Petting a cat the wrong way. The cat alleged willful misconduct and abuse—"

"But—but—but she was *purring*!"

"Just because she was purring doesn't mean she likes abuse. Guilty as charged."

You look up beseechingly to the judges. "What are my other crimes?"

"Being hit by an ambulance while in a crosswalk."

"But—but—but—" you say, "*They* hit *me* while *I* was in a crosswalk—"

"No excuse. Police personnel, fire department employees, Paramedics, city, county and state officers and workers, any official working for the Public Good and Order, building inspectors, pest control and all their agents, judges, accountants, corporate heads and trustees and members of the board thereof cannot be sued. You were in the wrong place at the wrong time. Guilty as charged."

You look up wonderingly. "Who *can* be sued?"

"Anyone else. Especially if you're poor, mentally ill, have no health insurance, don't speak English, are a woman or in a minority."

"That's an awful lot of people," you say.

"So?" says the judge in black.

"Mercy?" you try.

"Hahahahahahahaha," laugh the judges. "Guilty as charged."

The black-robed spider flings the carcass of the sucked-out fly at you and it lands with a moist *squarsh* on the table right in front of you. You sit there speechless. Then, as you dumbly wipe off fly guts, you realize you are indeed, fucked. Fucked big time. Fucked without end. Fucked like you never dreamed you could be fucked. Fucked without rhyme, without reason. Fucked without meaning to be fucked. Fucked beyond all comprehension. Fucked beyond your worst nightmare. Fucked like you've never believed it was possible to *be* fucked.

The white-robed judge snickers. "Wanna hear your sentence?"

You feel like your guts are caving in.

"Torture," says the judge. He takes a ball of silk and throws it at you; it hits you in the face and you are smothered. "Torture," says the judge, "I've always loved torture."

You wonder how this can possibly be justice.

"I bet you're wondering how this can possibly be justice," says the justice in white robes. "I'll tell you how it's justice. It makes me feel good to squash people like you who have no socially redeeming value by my standards. Your little miserable lives deserve to be snuffed out. That's the way it is. Some die, some win. Social Darwinism. Survival of the richest. Money equals power equals control. No money? No power. No power? No control. It's your fault. Wanna hear your punishment?"

You stand as if naked in the winds of the capricious order of things; standing before an existential firing squad who just sees this as another day, another paycheck and who could give a rat's ass about you. You're just target practice and that's *all* you are.

"Slow torture," says the spider judge, dressed in black, "by being dragged through hot coals, busted glass and then through a colony of fire ants."

"Then," says the judge in white robes, drooling, "we do it again. And again. And *again*. You will be given transplants and new skin to keep you alive *forever.*"

Oh, God, you think, *oh, God, this guy has read the Greeks—who was it that kept regrowing his liver again only to have it torn out by a vulture every night?*

Abruptly, your slimy lawyer friend is there beside you. "Well, looks like we lost. So it goes. Don't forget to pay your bill." Then, "Cheer up, it could be worse. You could be dead."

He slaps a bill down beside you for his services then scuttles off to God knows where. You don't even want to look at the bill but something at the bottom does catch your eye. A sentence in faded letters reads, "Your patronage is appreciated."

ACKNOWLEDGMENTS

All of the stories here reflect the superb editorial eye of a critique group which, as of this writing, has been meeting monthly for over two decades. None of my work goes out without the commentary and feedback of this group of people. I can never give these writers and friends the great respect and appreciation they deserve for making my writing the best it can possibly be. In regard to the critiquing of these stories in this volume, when they were written, the members whose feedback shaped these stories were, Marie Landis Edwards, Brian Herbert, Phyllis Hiefield, Linda Jean Shepherd, Ph. D., and Cal Clawson. The story, "The Infinite Tears of Pablo Azul", recently written, reflects the comments by newer members, Roberta Gregory and Sarah L. Blum, ARNP. Writers groups, when there is care and great respect given in feedback to the writer and story, can give anyone a tremendous advantage in an accurate assessment in one's growth as a writer and a professional. To this end, and how we've al endeavored to critique each other's work, as we, ourselves, would like to be critiqued—to paraphrase The Golden Rule—I have been so blessed. To the members who are no longer with the group as well as to the present members, I just want to say—thank you!

"Eggs," *Science Fiction Jahrbuch*, Moewig Science Fiction, Germany (1985)

"Justice in Amerry-Ka," *The Magazine of Bizarro Fiction #1* (2009)

"Insight," Alternate Realities Webzine, (2001)

"Safeway Passion," *Bumbershoot Anthology*, Writers in Performance (1981)

"Morality Play," *Continuum Science Fiction*, (Fall, 2005)

"Of Thumbs and Rafters," *Magic Realism, Vol IV.1* (Spring 1993)

"Planetary Loves," *ConAdian Souvenir Book*, The 52nd World Science Fiction Convention, (1994)

"Spiders," *Talebones*, (July, 1996)

ABOUT THE AUTHOR

Bruce Taylor, also know as "Mr. Magic Realism," was born in 1947 in Seattle, Washington, where he currently lives. He was a student at the Clarion West Science Fiction/Fantasy writing program at the University of Washington, with such writers as Robert Silverberg, Ursula K. LeGuin, Frank Herbert, and Harlan Ellison. He was Writer in Residence at Shakespeare & Company, Paris. He was a nominee for the &NOW Award for Innovative Writing and founder of the Magic Realist Writers International Network. His books include *Kafka's Uncle and Other Strange Tales*, *The Mountains of the Night*, *The Final Trick of Funnyman*, and *Edward: Dancing on the Edge of Infinity*. Bruce is co-editor, along with Elton Elliott, former editor of *The Science Fiction Review*, of the ground-breaking anthology, *Like Water For Quarks* which explores the blending of science fiction and magic realism. Visit him online at www.brucebtaylor.com.

Bizarro books

CATALOG   SPRING 2010

Bizarro Books publishes under the following imprints:

www.rawdogscreamingpress.com

www.eraserheadpress.com

www.afterbirthbooks.com

www.swallowdownpress.com

For all your Bizarro needs visit:

WWW.BIZARROCENTRAL.COM

Introduce yourselves to the bizarro genre and all of its authors with the Bizarro Starter Kit series. Each volume features short novels and short stories by ten of the leading bizarro authors, designed to give you a perfect sampling of the genre for only $5 plus shipping.

BB-0X1
"The Bizarro Starter Kit" (Orange)

Featuring D. Harlan Wilson, Carlton Mellick III, Jeremy Robert Johnson, Kevin L Donihe, Gina Ranalli, Andre Duza, Vincent W. Sakowski, Steve Beard, John Edward Lawson, and Bruce Taylor.

236 pages $5

BB-0X2
"The Bizarro Starter Kit" (Blue)

Featuring Ray Fracalossy, Jeremy C. Shipp, Jordan Krall, Mykle Hansen, Andersen Prunty, Eckhard Gerdes, Bradley Sands, Steve Aylett, Christian TeBordo, and Tony Rauch.

244 pages $5

BB-001 **"The Kafka Effekt" D. Harlan Wilson** - A collection of forty-four irreal short stories loosely written in the vein of Franz Kafka, with more than a pinch of William S. Burroughs sprinkled on top. **211 pages $14**

BB-002 **"Satan Burger" Carlton Mellick III** - The cult novel that put Carlton Mellick III on the map ... Six punks get jobs at a fast food restaurant owned by the devil in a city violently overpopulated by surreal alien cultures. **236 pages $14**

BB-003 **"Some Things Are Better Left Unplugged" Vincent Sakwoski** - Join The Man and his Nemesis, the obese tabby, for a nightmare roller coaster ride into this postmodern fantasy. **152 pages $10**

BB-004 **"Shall We Gather At the Garden?" Kevin L Donihe** - Donihe's Debut novel. Midgets take over the world, The Church of Lionel Richie vs. The Church of the Byrds, plant porn and more! **244 pages $14**

BB-005 **"Razor Wire Pubic Hair" Carlton Mellick III** - A genderless humandildo is purchased by a razor dominatrix and brought into her nightmarish world of bizarre sex and mutilation. **176 pages $11**

BB-006 **"Stranger on the Loose" D. Harlan Wilson** - The fiction of Wilson's 2nd collection is planted in the soil of normalcy, but what grows out of that soil is a dark, witty, otherworldly jungle... **228 pages $14**

BB-007 **"The Baby Jesus Butt Plug" Carlton Mellick III** - Using clones of the Baby Jesus for anal sex will be the hip sex fetish of the future. **92 pages $10**

BB-008 **"Fishyfleshed" Carlton Mellick III** - The world of the past is an illogical flatland lacking in dimension and color, a sick-scape of crispy squid people wandering the desert for no apparent reason. **260 pages $14**

BB-009 "Dead Bitch Army" Andre Duza - Step into a world filled with racist teenagers, cannibals, 100 warped Uncle Sams, automobiles with razor-sharp teeth, living graffiti, and a pissed-off zombie bitch out for revenge. **344 pages $16**

BB-010 "The Menstruating Mall" Carlton Mellick III - "The Breakfast Club meets Chopping Mall as directed by David Lynch." - Brian Keene **212 pages $12**

BB-011 "Angel Dust Apocalypse" Jeremy Robert Johnson - Meth-heads, man-made monsters, and murderous Neo-Nazis. "Seriously amazing short stories..." - Chuck Palahniuk, author of Fight Club **184 pages $11**

BB-012 "Ocean of Lard" Kevin L Donihe / Carlton Mellick III - A parody of those old Choose Your Own Adventure kid's books about some very odd pirates sailing on a sea made of animal fat. **176 pages $12**

BB-013 "Last Burn in Hell" John Edward Lawson - From his lurid angst-affair with a lesbian music diva to his ascendance as unlikely pop icon the one constant for Kenrick Brimley, official state prison gigolo, is he's got no clue what he's doing. **172 pages $14**

BB-014 "Tangerinephant" Kevin Dole 2 - TV-obsessed aliens have abducted Michael Tangerinephant in this bizarro combination of science fiction, satire, and surrealism. **164 pages $11**

BB-015 "Foop!" Chris Genoa - Strange happenings are going on at Dactyl, Inc, the world's first and only time travel tourism company.

"A surreal pie in the face!" - Christopher Moore **300 pages $14**

BB-016 "Spider Pie" Alyssa Sturgill - A one-way trip down a rabbit hole inhabited by sexual deviants and friendly monsters, fairytale beginnings and hideous endings. **104 pages $11**

BB-017 "The Unauthorized Woman" Efrem Emerson - Enter the world of the inner freak, a landscape populated by the pre-dead and morticioners, by cockroaches and 300-lb robots. **104 pages $11**

BB-018 "Fugue XXIX" Forrest Aguirre - Tales from the fringe of speculative literary fiction where innovative minds dream up the future's uncharted territories while mining forgotten treasures of the past. **220 pages $16**

BB-019 "Pocket Full of Loose Razorblades" John Edward Lawson - A collection of dark bizarro stories. From a giant rectum to a foot-fungus factory to a girl with a biforked tongue. **190 pages $13**

BB-020 "Punk Land" Carlton Mellick III - In the punk version of Heaven, the anarchist utopia is threatened by corporate fascism and only Goblin, Mortician's sperm, and a blue-mohawked female assassin named Shark Girl can stop them. **284 pages $15**

BB-021 "Pseudo-City" D. Harlan Wilson - Pseudo-City exposes what waits in the bathroom stall, under the manhole cover and in the corporate boardroom, all in a way that can only be described as mind-bogglingly irreal. **220 pages $16**

BB-022 "Kafka's Uncle and Other Strange Tales" Bruce Taylor - Anslenot and his giant tarantula (tormentor? fri-end?) wander a desecrated world in this novel and collection of stories from Mr. Magic Realism Himself. **348 pages $17**

BB-023 "Sex and Death In Television Town" Carlton Mellick III - In the old west, a gang of hermaphrodite gunslingers take refuge from a demon plague in Telos: a town where its citizens have televisions instead of heads. **184 pages $12**

BB-024 "It Came From Below The Belt" Bradley Sands - What can Grover Goldstein do when his severed, sentient penis forces him to return to high school and help it win the presidential election? **204 pages $13**

BB-025 "Sick: An Anthology of Illness" John Lawson, editor - These Sick stories are horrendous and hilarious dissections of creative minds on the scalpel's edge. **296 pages $16**

BB-026 "Tempting Disaster" John Lawson, editor - A shocking and alluring anthology from the fringe that examines our culture's obsession with taboos. **260 pages $16**

BB-027 "Siren Promised" Jeremy Robert Johnson & Alan M Clark - Nominated for the Bram Stoker Award. A potent mix of bad drugs, bad dreams, brutal bad guys, and surreal/incredible art by Alan M. Clark. **190 pages $13**

BB-028 "Chemical Gardens" Gina Ranalli - Ro and punk band Green is the Enemy find Kreepkins, a surfer-dude warlock, a vengeful demon, and a Metal Priestess in their way as they try to escape an underground nightmare. **188 pages $13**

BB-029 "Jesus Freaks" Andre Duza - For God so loved the world that he gave his only two begotten sons… and a few million zombies. **400 pages $16**

BB-030 "Grape City" Kevin L. Donihe - More Donihe-style comedic bizarro about a demon named Charles who is forced to work a minimum wage job on Earth after Hell goes out of business. **108 pages $10**

BB-031 "Sea of the Patchwork Cats" Carlton Mellick III - A quiet dreamlike tale set in the ashes of the human race. For Mellick enthusiasts who also adore The Twilight Zone. **112 pages $10**

BB-032 "Extinction Journals" Jeremy Robert Johnson - An uncanny voyage across a newly nuclear America where one man must confront the problems associated with loneliness, insane dieties, radiation, love, and an ever-evolving cockroach suit with a mind of its own. **104 pages $10**

BB-033 "Meat Puppet Cabaret" Steve Beard - At last! The secret connection between Jack the Ripper and Princess Diana's death revealed! **240 pages $16 / $30**

BB-034 "The Greatest Fucking Moment in Sports" Kevin L. Donihe - In the tradition of the surreal anti-sitcom Get A Life comes a tale of triumph and agape love from the master of comedic bizarro. **108 pages $10**

BB-035 "The Troublesome Amputee" John Edward Lawson - Disturbing verse from a man who truly believes nothing is sacred and intends to prove it. **104 pages $9**

BB-036 "Deity" Vic Mudd - God (who doesn't like to be called "God") comes down to a typical, suburban, Ohio family for a little vacation—but it doesn't turn out to be as relaxing as He had hoped it would be... **168 pages $12**

  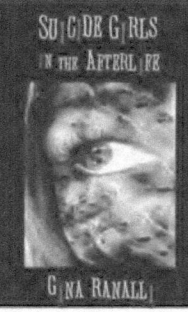 

BB-037 "The Haunted Vagina" Carlton Mellick III - It's difficult to love a woman whose vagina is a gateway to the world of the dead. **132 pages $10**

BB-038 "Tales from the Vinegar Wasteland" Ray Fracalossy - Witness: a man is slowly losing his face, a neighbor who periodically screams out for no apparent reason, and a house with a room that doesn't actually exist. **240 pages $14**

BB-039 "Suicide Girls in the Afterlife" Gina Ranalli - After Pogue commits suicide, she unexpectedly finds herself an unwilling "guest" at a hotel in the Afterlife, where she meets a group of bizarre characters, including a goth Satan, a hippie Jesus, and an alien-human hybrid. **100 pages $9**

BB-040 "And Your Point Is?" Steve Aylett - In this follow-up to LINT multiple authors provide critical commentary and essays about Jeff Lint's mind-bending literature. **104 pages $11**

BB-041 "Not Quite One of the Boys" Vincent Sakowski - While drug-dealer Maxi drinks with Dante in purgatory, God and Satan play a little tri-level chess and do a little bargaining over his business partner, Vinnie, who is still left on earth. **220 pages $14**

BB-042 "Teeth and Tongue Landscape" Carlton Mellick III - On a planet made out of meat, a socially-obsessive monophobic man tries to find his place amongst the strange creatures and communities that he comes across. **110 pages $10**

BB-043 "War Slut" Carlton Mellick III - Part "1984," part "Waiting for Godot," and part action horror video game adaptation of John Carpenter's "The Thing." **116 pages $10**

BB-044 "All Encompassing Trip" Nicole Del Sesto - In a world where coffee is no longer available, the only television shows are reality TV re-runs, and the animals are talking back, Nikki, Amber and a singing Coyote in a do-rag are out to restore the light   **308 pages $15**

BB-045 "Dr. Identity" D. Harlan Wilson - Follow the Dystopian Duo on a killing spree of epic proportions through the irreal postcapitalist city of Bliptown where time ticks sideways, artificial Bug-Eyed Monsters punish citizens for consumer-capitalist lethargy, and ultraviolence is as essential as a daily multivitamin. **208 pages $15**

BB-046 "The Million-Year Centipede" Eckhard Gerdes - Wakelin, frontman for 'The Hinge,' wrote a poem so prophetic that to ignore it dooms a person to drown in blood. **130 pages $12**

BB-047 "Sausagey Santa" Carlton Mellick III - A bizarro Christmas tale featuring Santa as a piratey mutant with a body made of sausages. 124 pages $10

BB-048 "Misadventures in a Thumbnail Universe" Vincent Sakowski - Dive deep into the surreal and satirical realms of neo-classical Blender Fiction, filled with television shoes and flesh-filled skies. **120 pages $10**

BB-049 **"Vacation" Jeremy C. Shipp** - Blueblood Bernard Johnson leaved his boring life behind to go on The Vacation, a year-long corporate sponsored odyssey. But instead of seeing the world, Bernard is captured by terrorists, becomes a key figure in secret drug wars, and, worse, doesn't once miss his secure American Dream. **160 pages $14**

BB-051 **"13 Thorns" Gina Ranalli** - Thirteen tales of twisted, bizarro horror. **240 pages $13**

BB-050 **"Discouraging at Best" John Edward Lawson** - A collection where the absurdity of the mundane expands exponentially creating a tidal wave that sweeps reason away. For those who enjoy satire, bizarro, or a good old-fashioned slap to the senses. **208 pages $15**

BB-052 **"Better Ways of Being Dead" Christian TeBordo** - In this class, the students have to keep one palm down on the table at all times, and listen to lectures about a panda who speaks Chinese. **216 pages $14**

BB-053 **"Ballad of a Slow Poisoner" Andrew Goldfarb** Millford Mutterwurst sat down on a Tuesday to take his afternoon tea, and made the unpleasant discovery that his elbows were becoming flatter. **128 pages $10**

BB-054 **"Wall of Kiss" Gina Ranalli** - A woman... A wall... Sometimes love blooms in the strangest of places. **108 pages $9**

BB-055 **"HELP! A Bear is Eating Me" Mykle Hansen** - The bizarro, heartwarming, magical tale of poor planning, hubris and severe blood loss... **150 pages $11**

BB-056 **"Piecemeal June" Jordan Krall** - A man falls in love with a living sex doll, but with love comes danger when her creator comes after her with crab-squid assassins. **90 pages $9**

BB-057 **"Laredo" Tony Rauch** - Dreamlike, surreal stories by Tony Rauch. **180 pages $12**

BB-058 **"The Overwhelming Urge" Andersen Prunty** - A collection of bizarro tales by Andersen Prunty. **150 pages $11**

BB-059 **"Adolf in Wonderland" Carlton Mellick III** - A dreamlike adventure that takes a young descendant of Adolf Hitler's design and sends him down the rabbit hole into a world of imperfection and disorder. **180 pages $11**

BB-060 **"Super Cell Anemia" Duncan B. Barlow** - "Unrelentingly bizarre and mysterious, unsettling in all the right ways..." - Brian Evenson. **180 pages $12**

BB-061 **"Ultra Fuckers" Carlton Mellick III** - Absurdist suburban horror about a couple who enter an upper middle class gated community but can't find their way out. **108 pages $9**

BB-062 **"House of Houses" Kevin L. Donihe** - An odd man wants to marry his house. Unfortunately, all of the houses in the world collapse at the same time in the Great House Holocaust. Now he must travel to House Heaven to find his departed fiancee. **172 pages $11**

BB-063 **"Necro Sex Machine" Andre Duza** - The Dead Bitch returns in this follow-up to the bizarro zombie epic Dead Bitch Army. **400 pages $16**

BB-064 **"Squid Pulp Blues" Jordan Krall** - In these three bizarro-noir novellas, the reader is thrown into a world of murderers, drugs made from squid parts, deformed gun-toting veterans, and a mischievous apocalyptic donkey. **204 pages $12**

BB-065 **"Jack and Mr. Grin" Andersen Prunty** - "When Mr. Grin calls you can hear a smile in his voice. Not a warm and friendly smile, but the kind that seizes your spine in fear. You don't need to pay your phone bill to hear it. That smile is in every line of Prunty's prose." - Tom Bradley. **208 pages $12**

BB-066 **"Cybernetrix" Carlton Mellick III** - What would you do if your normal everyday world was slowly mutating into the video game world from Tron? **212 pages $12**

BB-067 **"Lemur" Tom Bradley** - Spencer Sproul is a would-be serial-killing bus boy who can't manage to murder, injure, or even scare anybody. However, there are other ways to do damage to far more people and do it legally... **120 pages $12**

BB-068 **"Cocoon of Terror" Jason Earls** - Decapitated corpses...a sculpture of terror...Zelian's masterpiece, his Cocoon of Terror, will trigger a supernatural disaster for everyone on Earth. **196 pages $14**

BB-069 **"Mother Puncher" Gina Ranalli** - The world has become tragically over-populated and now the government strongly opposes procreation. Ed is employed by the government as a mother-puncher. He doesn't relish his job, but he knows it has to be done and he knows he's the best one to do it. **120 pages $9**

BB-070 **"My Landlady the Lobotomist" Eckhard Gerdes** - The brains of past tenants line the shelves of my boarding house, soaking in a mysterious elixir. One more slip-up and the landlady might just add my frontal lobe to her collection. **116 pages $12**

BB-071 **"CPR for Dummies" Mickey Z.** - This hilarious freakshow at the world's end is the fragmented, sobering debut novel by acclaimed nonfiction author Mickey Z. **216 pages $14**

BB-072 **"Zerostrata" Andersen Prunty** - Hansel Nothing lives in a tree house, suffers from memory loss, has a very eccentric family, and falls in love with a woman who runs naked through the woods every night. **144 pages $11**

BB-073 **"The Egg Man" Carlton Mellick III** - It is a world where humans reproduce like insects. Children are the property of corporations, and having an enormous ten-foot brain implanted into your skull is a grotesque sexual fetish. Mellick's industrial urban dystopia is one of his darkest and grittiest to date. **184 pages $11**

BB-074 **"Shark Hunting in Paradise Garden" Cameron Pierce** - A group of strange humanoid religious fanatics travel back in time to the Garden of Eden to discover it is invested with hundreds of giant flying maneating sharks. **150 pages $10**

BB-075 **"Apeshit" Carlton Mellick III** - Friday the 13th meets Visitor Q. Six hipster teens go to a cabin in the woods inhabited by a deformed killer. An incredibly fucked-up parody of B-horror movies with a bizarro slant. **192 pages $12**

BB-076 **"Rampaging Fuckers of Everything on the Crazy Shitting Planet of the Vomit At smosphere" Mykle Hansen** - 3 bizarro satires. Monster Cocks, Journey to the Center of Agnes Cuddlebottom, and Crazy Shitting Planet. **228 pages $12**

BB-077 **"The Kissing Bug" Daniel Scott Buck** - In the tradition of Roald Dahl, Tim Burton, and Edward Gorey, comes this bizarro anti-war children's story about a bohemian conenose kissing bug who falls in love with a human woman. **116 pages $10**

BB-078 **"MachoPoni" Lotus Rose** - It's My Little Pony... *Bizarro* style! A long time ago Poniworld was split in two. On one side of the Jagged Line is the Pastel Kingdom, a magical land of music, parties, and positivity. On the other side of the Jagged Line is Dark Kingdom inhabited by an army of undead ponies. **148 pages $11**

BB-079 **"The Faggiest Vampire" Carlton Mellick III** - A Roald Dahlesque children's story about two faggy vampires who partake in a mustache competition to find out which one is truly the faggiest. **104 pages $10**

BB-080 **"Sky Tongues" Gina Ranalli** - The autobiography of Sky Tongues, the biracial hermaphrodite actress with tongues for fingers. Follow her strange life story as she rises from freak to fame. **204 pages $12**

BB-081 **"Washer Mouth" Kevin L. Donihe** - A washing machine becomes human and pursues his dream of meeting his favorite soap opera star. **244 pages $11**

BB-082 **"Shatnerquake" Jeff Burk** - All of the characters ever played by William Shatner are suddenly sucked into our world. Their mission: hunt down and destroy the real William Shatner. **100 pages $10**

BB-083 **"The Cannibals of Candyland" Carlton Mellick III** - There exists a race of cannibals that are made of candy. They live in an underground world made out of candy. One man has dedicated his life to killing them all. **170 pages $11**

BB-084 **"Slub Glub in the Weird World of the Weeping Willows" Andrew Goldfarb** - The charming tale of a blue glob named Slub Glub who helps the weeping willows whose tears are flooding the earth. There are also hyenas, ghosts, and a voodoo priest **100 pages $10**

BB-085 **"Super Fetus" Adam Pepper** - Try to abort this fetus and he'll kick your ass! **104 pages $10**

BB-086 **"Fistful of Feet" Jordan Krall** - A bizarro tribute to spaghetti westerns, featuring Cthulhu-worshipping Indians, a woman with four feet, a crazed gunman who is obsessed with sucking on candy, Syphilis-ridden mutants, sexually transmitted tattoos, and a house devoted to the freakiest fetishes. **228 pages $12**

BB-087 **"Ass Goblins of Auschwitz" Cameron Pierce** - It's Monty Python meets Nazi exploitation in a surreal nightmare as can only be imagined by Bizarro author Cameron Pierce. **104 pages $10**

BB-088 **"Silent Weapons for Quiet Wars" Cody Goodfellow** - "This is high-end psychological surrealist horror meets bottom-feeding low-life crime in a techno-thrilling science fiction world full of Lovecraft and magic..." -John Skipp **212 pages $12**

BB-089 "Warrior Wolf Women of the Wasteland" Carlton Mellick III
Road Warrior Werewolves versus McDonaldland Mutants...post-apocalyptic fiction has never been quite like this. **316 pages $13**

BB-090 "Cursed" Jeremy C Shipp - The story of a group of characters who believe they are cursed and attempt to figure out who cursed them and why. A tale of stylish absurdism and suspenseful horror. **218 pages $15**

BB-091 "Super Giant Monster Time" Jeff Burk - A tribute to choose your own adventures and Godzilla movies. Will you escape the giant monsters that are rampaging the fuck out of your city and shit? Or will you join the mob of alien-controlled punk rockers causing chaos in the streets? What happens next depends on you. **188 pages $12**

BB-092 "Perfect Union" Cody Goodfellow - "Cronenberg's THE FLY on a grand scale: human/insect gene-spliced body horror, where the human hive politics are as shocking as the gore." -John Skipp. **272 pages $13**

BB-093 "Sunset with a Beard" Carlton Mellick III - 14 stories of surreal science fiction. **200 pages $12**

BB-094 "My Fake War" Andersen Prunty - The absurd tale of an unlikely soldier forced to fight a war that, quite possibly, does not exist. It's Rambo meets Waiting for Godot in this subversive satire of American values and the scope of the human imagination. **128 pages $11**

BB-095 "Lost in Cat Brain Land" Cameron Pierce - Sad stories from a surreal world. A fascist mustache, the ghost of Franz Kafka, a desert inside a dead cat. Primordial entities mourn the death of their child. The desperate serve tea to mysterious creatures. A hopeless romantic falls in love with a pterodactyl. And much more. **152 pages $11**

BB-096 "The Kobold Wizard's Dildo of Enlightenment +2" Carlton Mellick III - A Dungeons and Dragons parody about a group of people who learn they are only made up characters in an AD&D campaign and must find a way to resist their nerdy teenaged players and retarded dungeon master in order to survive. 232 **pages $12**

ORDER FORM

TITLES	QTY	PRICE	TOTAL

Please make checks and moneyorders payable to ROSE O'KEEFE / BIZARRO BOOKS in U.S. funds only. Please don't send bad checks! Allow 2-6 weeks for delivery. International orders may take longer. If you'd like to pay online via PAYPAL.COM, send payments to publisher@eraserheadpress.com.

SHIPPING: US ORDERS - $2 for the first book, $1 for each additional book. For priority shipping, add an additional $4. INT'L ORDERS - $5 for the first book, $3 for each additional book. Add an additional $5 per book for global priority shipping.

Send payment to:

BIZARRO BOOKS
 C/O Rose O'Keefe
 205 NE Bryant
 Portland, OR 97211

Address

City   State   Zip

Email   Phone